A SIMPLE COUNTRY FUNERAL

BLYTHE BAKER

~

Death returns to the country ...

A quite country life continues to elude Helen Lightholder, as she wrestles with her recent bereavement. When the grisly murder of a nameless vagabond shocks the local community, Helen sets out to unearth the truth behind the inexplicable killing.

But Bookminster hides secrets almost as old as it's 14th century market place, and the village's inhabitants will do anything to thwart a prying outsider. Helen's snooping at a convalescent home for wounded soldiers leads to an apparent dead end, even as other obstacles loom in her path. With Inspector Graves blocking her investigation at every turn and a mysterious, shadowy figure continuing to dog her steps, can Helen unmask the most dangerous killer she has ever faced?

~

1

——

"**Y**ou're very welcome. Have a splendid day," I said, smiling at the elderly couple sitting at the table beside the window.

I turned with a tray laden with empty teacups and bowls of sugar cubes, making my way through the mismatched tables and chairs of the tea shop. The happy hum of conversation filled my ears, and the spiced scent of freshly baked cinnamon bread filtered in from the kitchens.

I leaned against the swinging door leading out of the shop, whistling as I stepped into the kitchen.

The steam of the kitchen greeted me as soon as I entered. Kettles boiled merrily on the stove, and the oven glowed with a deep, rich red where I knew fresh, delicious treats were being baked for the guests.

"Mr. and Mrs. Smith are leaving," I said, setting the tray down on the countertop beside the sink. I reached into the front pocket of my apron, pulling out a few shillings. "They left a rather generous tip today, though."

"Oh, good heavens..." Irene said, brushing some of her thick, blonde hair from her eyesight with her arm; her hands were covered in frothy bubbles from the hot water bath she was soaking the cups and pots in as she washed them. "I told them they didn't need to do that anymore. I'm worried they won't have enough to get by themselves..."

"He keeps saying that all he wants is for us to be able to have something nice," I said. "Especially your son."

Irene shook her head. "Well...it is very kind of them, but I just wish they would listen to me."

"How long have they been customers here?" I asked, rolling up the sleeves of my blouse and dousing my hands in the hot, soapy water. I swept my hands around the bottom of the basin until I found a rag, and began to scrub at one of the cups I'd brought in with me before passing it over to Irene.

"Since we opened," she said, taking the cup from my dripping hand. "And they have been here almost every day since. All except the day that Mrs. Smith was so ill that they needed to take her all the way into London. The nearer hospital couldn't help her."

"How awful," I said.

"She is a strong woman, and she recovered quickly," Irene said with a smile. "You know, Helen, I really must thank you again for being willing to come in and help me on your day off. With Nathanial being away, I just needed the extra set of hands in here to ensure I could keep up with all the customers and their orders."

"It really is no trouble," I said. "When I said that I was

happy to help whenever you needed me, I meant it, you know."

Irene smiled appreciatively at me. "You really are too kind," she said.

We worked to quickly finish the rest of the dishes, making quick work of them together. I set the clean cups up on the shelf alongside all the others, ready for the next customers to arrive.

"So..." Irene asked, turning her scrutinizing grey eyes on me. "How have you been feeling?"

I wiped my hands dry on the apron tied around my waist, frowning at her. "Whatever do you mean? I feel perfectly fine."

Irene shook her head, folding her arms. "You know what I mean. How are you feeling about...well, everything, really."

I shifted my gaze to the floor, the sound of the steam rising from a teapot drawing my attention. I moved quickly to the stove to remove it before it boiled over.

"You went through a very traumatic experience just a few short weeks ago," Irene said in a very concerned tone. "Something that no one should ever have to experience... and so soon after losing Roger."

My heart clenched with hearing the name of my late husband being said so frankly by someone who had never known him. In many ways, however, my friendship with Irene felt as if it had lasted for years.

"I know how difficult it is for you to talk about these things that have happened, but it is not something you should have to carry around all on your own," she said, her brow creasing with concern. "Has talking about Roger like I suggested helped at all?"

"Yes," I said. "Surprisingly, it has. It certainly wasn't easy the first few times, but it made me realize that I think I will be able to have a future...even if it is vastly different from the one I expected to have."

"That's good," Irene said. "Very good."

I poured the steaming water into a pale blue ceramic teapot, ready to be taken out to customers. "When it comes to what happened a few weeks ago...I am still not quite sure how to process it all. I have spent many nights trying to decide if there was a different way for everything to have happened, and I...I just cannot seem to find a solution that did not end in her attacking me."

Irene nodded, yet her expression seemed rather frightened.

"I know for certain that if Sidney Mason had not been there, she would have killed me," I said.

The words hung in the air, suspended between us, heavy like clouds swelling with rain.

"Well, we cannot allow ourselves to dwell on that," Irene said. "It didn't happen, and all we can do is be thankful for it."

"I know..." I said. "It's just incredibly hard to believe that someone could be so wicked, so completely wrapped up in themselves that they would hurt someone else so thoughtlessly...it just doesn't make any sense."

"I know," Irene said. "The world is full of cruel people. But there are many people who are like you, Helen. Thoughtful. Caring. Compassionate. People like you would never be able to do that to others."

"No," I said. "I never could. Taking another person's life..."

The death of Mrs. Sandra Martin had struck Brookminster rather hard. Everyone knew her, and while it was clear that many people were not all that fond of her, no one could find anything bad to say about her in the days following her passing.

Sidney Mason, however, had become quite the hero around town. I had been worried that he would have been arrested for being the one to pull the trigger of the gun that had killed Sandra. It was clear, though, to everyone who had come to the shop that day that his actions had been taken in defense of both himself and of me.

I still felt rather ashamed that I had ever thought that Sidney might have been mixed up in the nonsense going on with my aunt.

"Well...there's no need to dwell on it for too long, today," Irene said. "Would you care to go out and check on our guests? See if anyone else has come in?"

"Of course," I said. "Shall I deliver the cinnamon bread to Mrs. Trent?"

"It should be done, yes," Irene said, glancing over her shoulder at the oven behind her. "That's quite fragrant now. Maybe give it just another minute more."

I wasn't sure I would ever understand Irene's innate ability to just know when anything in the oven was done baking, but I hoped to someday be able to learn even a fraction of her skills.

I scooped the warm, heavenly bread from the oven, and carried it out into the dining area, still steaming.

"I'm sorry for the wait, Mrs. Trent," I said, smiling at the sweet faced old woman who was sitting in her usual corner beside the grandfather clock. I set the bread down on the table, picking up the knife from the opposite place setting. "The bread just finished."

"Oh, that's all right, dear," Mrs. Trent said, her expression kind and gentle. "There's nothing to worry about. I was rather pleased to just sit here and enjoy my tea."

"Well, allow me to top you off, then," said Irene, who had followed me out into the dining area. She lifted the teapot I had just filled in the kitchen, and tipped it over Mrs. Trent's teacup.

There weren't many customers at this time, and the other two couples that were there were happily chatting, unaware of our presence.

"Would you like one slice of bread? Or two?" I asked.

"Just one for now," Mrs. Trent said.

"And sugar?" Irene asked.

"A little, yes," Mrs. Trent said.

Irene took a step back, holding her tray against her chest. 'So, Mrs. Trent. How is your husband doing? Is he feeling any better?"

"Oh, yes," Mrs. Trent said, pulling off a corner of the steaming bread, releasing its heady scent into the air. "He is home now, of course. Enjoying all the comforts afforded to him."

"Is Dr. Vaughn making house calls now?" Irene asked.

Mrs. Trent nodded. "Indeed. And I am grateful for his care, as well, especially since he has been spending so many of his working hours over at the Evermore estate."

"Really?" Irene asked, her brow furrowing. "What has he been doing over there? Is Lord Evermore ill?"

"You haven't heard?" Mrs. Trent asked, her eyes widening. "Why, Evermore estate has been turned over to be used by the military. London's hospitals are full up with wounded soldiers, and there has apparently been a serious need for beds for the wounded soldiers."

"My gracious…" Irene said.

"They've given up their whole home for the wounded?" I asked, rather astonished.

Mrs. Trent nodded. "Indeed. Lord Evermore is quite good friends with Dr. Vaughn, and thought nothing of giving him the chance to see patients close to home. There was no earthly way they could have brought more than a half a dozen to his little surgery here in town. There, though, they shall be comfortable, and their recovery will hopefully be rapid."

"Not only that, but I imagine it's a much cleaner environment than some of those military hospitals…" Irene said, suppressing a shudder. "I have heard some terrible stories about how those poor soldiers are treated."

"As have I," Mrs. Trent said. "I've heard tales of rats living in the same rooms as the patients, and all the sickness they bring along with them…"

"That certainly won't be a problem at a private estate," Irene said. "That was very kind of the Evermores to open their home for the benefit of the wounded."

"It certainly was," Mrs. Trent said. "I imagine those soldiers will be much more relaxed here than they ever would have been in London or Bath."

"Are there many patients there now?" I asked, cutting

another slice of the cinnamon bread for Mrs. Trent, who had already consumed most of hers as she tore small chunks of it off.

"Quite a few, yes," Mrs. Trent said. "According to Dr. Vaughn, they have more than two dozen set up currently, and are expecting to receive even more in the coming weeks."

"This war is a terrible thing," Irene said in a low, quiet voice. "I wish it would just end."

"As do I," Mrs. Trent said. "I'm worried about Mr. Trent; our nephew, Thomas, was sent overseas. I believe he is in Poland."

"Poland?" Irene asked. "I didn't realize there were any soldiers still there. I was under the impression we had pulled out from there some time ago."

"We aren't quite sure what Thomas is doing, but we know that he cannot discuss much of his work," Mrs. Trent said, pushing her glasses up the bridge of her slender nose. "He is not at liberty to divulge that information. Nevertheless, my poor husband is worried sick over the boy. Thinks he will receive that dreaded phone call from his sister any day now..."

"That's certainly not good for his health," Irene said.

"I've told him as much," Mrs. Trent said. "The best we can do now is hope and pray for his safe return. Apart from that, it is entirely out of our control..."

I swallowed hard, picking up the rest of the cinnamon bread from the table.

Not knowing what he was up to, knowing he was not at liberty to discuss it, felt far too familiar.

I was well aware of the fact that my late husband had

not been the only one with a secret job, with secret goals. But it still hurt my heart to hear that these men were having to erect barriers between themselves and their families, their dearest loved ones, in order to further the war.

It troubled me deeply, and as so many things had since the end of February, I was reminded of Roger and the life we had taken from us so soon.

"Are you all right?" Irene asked, following me back into the kitchens. "A crestfallen expression came over you while we were talking with Mrs. Trent."

"I'm..." I said, catching myself as I realized I had very nearly said everything was just fine. I sighed, gathering my thoughts once again. "I was just thinking that Mrs. Trent's nephew reminded me of Roger is all."

"Because of his rather vague job?" she asked.

I nodded. "There is still a part of me that wishes I knew what he did, or what he had been doing, when he died. I know it was important work, whatever it was, but I still worry that there was a great deal about him that I didn't know...that I will never know."

"Oh, sweetheart..." Irene said, coming over to me and wrapping her arms around me. "You knew him. Just because you didn't know precisely everything he did, doesn't mean that you didn't know *him*. You knew his heart, and you knew his love for you. And from what you've told me about him, he never would have kept everything he did from you if he didn't absolutely have to."

"I suppose you're right," I said.

"Good," Irene said. "Now, I believe you have helped

me enough today. Why don't you run along home, and get some rest?"

"But what about the other customers? Won't you need my help?" I asked.

"With Mrs. Trent and the engrossed love birds? I think I can manage just fine," she said with a smile and a wink. "Besides, didn't you have some orders that you needed to fill for your own shop?"

My face flushed, my heart skipping a beat. "Oh. Yes, you're right. I suppose I should be on my way."

I hung up my apron on the back of the swinging kitchen door, a small, paper bag filled with some slices of Irene's cinnamon bread tucked inside my purse.

"Have a wonderful rest of your day," Irene said from beside Mrs. Trent's table, another fresh pot of tea in her hands. "I'll see you tomorrow!"

"You as well!" I said, smiling as I stepped out into the warm, summer air.

June had greeted Brookminster with warmth and comfort. The rains seemed to have dissipated somewhat, leaving us with more sunny days than miserable, gloomy ones.

As I stepped outside into the beautiful day, I inhaled deeply, breathing in the scent of the freshly blooming flowers.

"Mrs. Lightholder," I heard behind me. "Wait up!"

2

I turned around at the familiar voice, which was both unexpected, yet pleasing to hear.

"Sidney Mason," I said, smiling at the young man hurrying toward me up the road. "What a pleasant surprise."

Sidney Mason was a fairly young man, no more than thirty, with fiery red hair and a face full of freckles. His eyes were wide and bright, and his smile as warm as the sunshine on my face.

"I thought that might have been you," he said in his Scots accent, coming to a stop beside me. He tore the hat from his head and gave me a rather quick bow. "You and Irene are becoming thick as thieves, aren't you?"

I smiled. "And what if we are?" I asked, starting back down the road toward home.

"Well, I certainly can think of no other woman who would take care of you so well," Sidney said. "You know, I was there helping her husband repair their washing machine last week, and she not only asked me to stay for dinner, but she sent me home with the leftovers, too."

I grinned. "That certainly sounds like Irene, yes."

"She is perhaps the most generous person I have ever known," Sidney said. "Well, you are generous yourself, Miss Helen. I'm still quite taken with that biscuit recipe of yours."

"Did you like them?" I asked. "I thought to try oats ground up in the batter instead of using so much flour."

"And the chocolate?" he added, nodding his head. "It was excellent. I could have happily eaten those all day. I rationed myself, though, as we all must in these trying times."

"I'm surprised," I said. "That chocolate was from a single bar I purchased at the sweets shop. I thought I might treat myself."

"And you shared it with me?" he asked. "I'm honored."

"Well, since you won't accept any sort of money for the things I have asked you to take care of for me..." I said, smiling at him.

He gave me a sheepish look. "I couldn't possibly ask for money from you," he said. "As I've told you, time and again, I do it because I'm happy to do so. I enjoy it. The reward is the work itself, you see?"

I laughed, shaking my head. "You are quite the character, Mr. Mason."

"Sidney," he corrected with a smile. "You know, your hair seems a bit lighter than usual," he added. "Though, of course, you have been spending a great deal of time in your garden. That would certainly explain those strands of honey gold in your lovely, dark hair."

My heart fluttered, and I reached up to touch the ends of my hair, which I had just had cut a few days prior. "You think so?" I asked, examining it. For the first time, I did notice the warmer tones mixed throughout the chocolatey browns. "Perhaps I have been."

"How are those vegetables growing, eh?" he asked. "You've planted a good variety back there."

"Yes," I said. "They seem to be doing well. In fact, the tomatoes should be ripe in just a few days. Maybe I will make some soup, or even stewed tomatoes for breakfast."

"Careful not to say that too loudly," Sidney said with a smirk. "Otherwise I shall be at your door, knocking hopefully, tempted by the delicious smells."

We laughed as we rounded the corner of High Street, our houses that stood side by side coming into view further down the street.

Sidney had been a wonderful neighbor. Not only was he available nearly any time I needed his help with something, but he had gone far above and beyond any sort of friendly action by creating useful items for me, such as the planter boxes I was now using in my garden, as well as a new shelving unit for all the books I had no place for in my flat.

"How is that truck of yours?" I asked.

"Oh, you mean my newest pet project?" he asked, shifting the paper bag he carried in his arm to the other. "It's going well, actually. I know it must have been difficult for Mrs. Georgianna to part with her husband's truck, but she had no interest in trying to get it running again. Apparently, it had sat in their garage for almost six years. I guess he just kept putting it off, saying over and over that he would start fixing it up the next weekend."

"Did he pass away before he ever got around to it?" I asked.

He nodded. "Yes. That's precisely what happened. To be honest, I think she was pleased to be rid of the thing. Too many painful memories."

"I can understand that..." I said. "After my husband passed away, I couldn't stand the sight of his clothing hanging in my closet. There was something deeply unsettling about the fact that he had, at one point, worn them, but never would again..." I shook my head. "I don't know. Perhaps that doesn't make much sense."

"No, it does," Sidney said. "I can imagine it must have hurt to think of everything that might have been, but never could be now."

"Yes..." I said. "Just that."

We walked in silence for a moment, our footsteps and the chirping of the summer birds filling the void.

"I suppose you must miss him," he said, in a low voice.

"I do," I said. "All the time."

"I'm sorry," Sidney said.

"It's all right," I said. "It gets a little easier every day."

"I'm glad to hear it," he said.

I smiled at him, but noticed his expression change to surprise as he stared at something over my shoulder.

"What is it?" I asked.

Apparent concern caused his brow to furrow. In one

swift movement, Sidney gently laid a hand on my arm, and stepped around me.

"What's going on?" I asked.

It only took me one glance to understand what he was looking at.

A man was standing along the side of the road, leaning against the stone wall that separated the front gardens of some of the homes along High Street. He seemed to be holding onto it for support, leaning primarily on his left leg.

He wore a tattered coat with patches in the elbows, and trousers that had a hem several centimeters too short. His shoes looked as if the soles were worn all the way down, with scuffs along the toes and heels.

I was barely able to see him over Sidney's shoulder, but it was clear from Sidney's straightened back and stiff shoulders that he found this man troubling.

I wasn't going to object to his intercession if the stranger ended up being the vagabond he looked to be.

However, the man did not strike me as terribly threatening. He swayed slightly as he turned his gaze onto us, and took a step in our direction.

"'Ello?" he said, plucking the tattered hat from the top of his head.

Sidney glanced over his shoulder at me briefly. "Just stay behind me, I'll talk to him," he said.

I nodded. Who was this stranger? What did he want?

"Good afternoon, sir," Sidney said with a polite wave. "Can I help you with something?"

The man opened his mouth and replied, but it was not in English. It was some language that I was not all that familiar with. It was harsh, though, with guttural sounds and hard stops.

He was speaking rapidly, moving his hands wildly in the air; he pointed up the street, scratched the side of his head, and replaced his hat on his head.

"Sir, sir, please," Sidney said, his voice rising in volume and slowing in speed. He held his hands up in front of himself in caution. "I'm sorry, but I do not understand what you are saying. Do you speak English?"

The man stopped, his mouth hanging open.

For a brief moment, his gaze shifted over to me, before returning to Sidney.

"Little," the man said. "English." His accent was thick, even around the words.

"All right, good," Sidney said, relaxing somewhat. "Now, are you trying to find a certain place? Or perhaps someone?"

The man nodded, and took off in another speech in his native language.

"Sir, it's all right," Sidney said, attempting to speak over the man's frantic babbling. "I can help you. You just need to tell me what it is you are looking for. As best you can."

The man stared at Sidney, searching his face. For a moment, I wondered if he perhaps hadn't understood anything Sidney had said to him.

He said a single word in his language, pointing at his chest. "Need find," he said.

"Yes, I know," Sidney said. "But what do you need to find?"

The man's brow furrowed, and he repeated the word.

Sidney shook his head. "I'm sorry, but I don't know what that means."

The man scratched his chin, and as he turned his head and looked around, I saw the gauntness in his face.

"This poor man..." I said, just under my breath to Sidney. "When was the last time he's eaten anything?"

The man pulled the hat off his head again, and his eyes fell on me once more. He pointed at me.

I pointed at myself, and Sidney's eyes moved to me.

"Me?" I asked.

The man shook his head. "Kobieta."

"Ko...what does he mean?" I asked.

A spark flickered in Sidney's eyes. "Do you mean...a woman? A lady?" Sidney asked, pointing once again to me.

The man's face split into a wide smile, and he nodded. "Kobieta."

Sidney glanced over his shoulder at me. "He's looking for someone. Maybe a daughter? Or a wife?"

My heart ached for him suddenly. "Well, we can't very well help him like this," I said. "He needs someone who speaks his own language."

"You're right..." Sidney said. "I suppose we could send him over to the police station. Maybe someone there might be able to help him – "

"I'm not certain he'd get much help there..." I said, dropping my voice. I glanced over at the man once again. He seemed to be watching us and our conversation carefully. "Isn't he – " I said, my heart skipping. "Isn't he a German?"

Sidney shrugged. "I thought he might have been at

first, too, but I believe he's a Polish refugee." Sidney looked over at the man. "You're from Poland, aren't you?"

The man nodded. "Yah," he said. "Polska."

Sidney smiled. "See?"

"How did you know that?" I asked.

"One of my very good friends is Polish," Sidney said. His face fell, though. "...I certainly hope he got out before..."

He didn't have to finish his sentence.

"Sir, we would like to help you find this woman you are looking for," Sidney said, slowly and concisely. "What does she look like?" he asked, gesturing to the whole of his face.

The man nodded. "Ah, tall," he said, measuring a height just beneath his own. He pointed at his hair, and then pointed over at me. "Hair dark," he said. "Good?"

"Well, it's a start," Sidney said. "Sir, do you have a place to stay?" He put his hands together and rested them against his chin as if he were sleeping.

"Sleep?" the man asked. He shook his head, pointing down the street. "Kobieta, woman," he said.

"He's so determined to find her that he hasn't stopped," Sidney said.

That hurt my heart to think about. I stared over at the man, seeing the hope in his expression. How many miles had he traveled, looking for this woman?

Sidney took a step forward, reaching into the bag in his arms

"Here," he said, pulling out a small loaf of bread and a slab of hard cheese, presumably his own lunch. He offered them to the man. "You should take this. Have something to eat."

The man's lips parted, and he seemed dumbfounded as he looked between Sidney and the food. "Food?" he asked.

Sidney nodded. "For you."

The man hesitantly stepped toward us, ever so slowly reaching out for the food. He reminded me of a stray dog being offered a meal, terrified to trust, lest he be attacked.

Sidney pulled out some money from his pocket, as well, and offered that, too.

The man, seeing the money, stepped backward, shaking his head.

"It's all right," Sidney said. "That food won't last forever."

Sidney ended up convincing the man to take both the food, and the money. "I am going to take him down to the police station," Sidney said to me. "Hopefully someone there will be able to do something for him."

"Are you certain that's the best choice?" I asked.

"I can't think of any others," Sidney said. "There aren't many Polish families outside of London that I'm aware of, and many of them are refugees, fleeing the war...much like this man and the woman he is looking for must be."

I nodded. "I suppose you're right. Well, I hope they can do something for him. I hope someone there will have the patience to try and communicate with him."

"Precisely," Sidney said. He then turned back to the man, who was eyeing the cheese with a hungry expression. "All right there, sir. Let's head down to the police station. See if we can't get you some help."

The man nodded, and he smiled over at me.

I returned the smile, watching the two men walk back up High Street the way Sidney and I had come.

I did hope that poor man could find some help.

As I started for home, I realized my heart was heavy. War was a terrible thing, forcing people to open their homes as hospitals for wounded soldiers, while families like that of the poor Polish man were ripped apart.

One day soon, though...we all hoped the war would be over. The nightmares would finally stop, and life could return to some semblance of normalcy.

But what would that normal look like? Everyone knew someone that was lost in this horrible fight. How could we ever hope to carry on living when they were gone?

We must. That was all there was to it.

And maybe, someday...we might learn to find peace amidst all the pain.

3

"Yes, Mother, I assure you...everything is perfectly fine," I said for what felt like the tenth time that hour.

"You keep saying that, and yet you don't call, you don't write," said the voice of my mother on the other end of the telephone. "Have you thought about coming home? Even for a short visit? Your father's birthday is in a few weeks, I know he would love to see you."

"I would very much like to," I said as I separated and organized yet another mismatched box of buttons by color and shape. "But I have my hands full with this shop. If I were to leave, even for a few days, I would have some very upset customers."

"Surely people can live without ribbons and pins for a short amount of time," she said with disdain.

I sighed, closing my eyes for a moment, trying my best to gather the little patience I had left. "I know that you miss me. And I miss you both, too. But this move has been good for me, and to be honest, I am very happy here in Brookminster. I am making friends, and am slowly getting used to running a business all on my own..." Not to mention that I was starting to heal, *finally,* after all these months. "For the first time, I am beginning to find peace."

Now it was my mother's turn to sigh. "I understand," she said. "And I am glad for you, sweetheart. I truly am. I just hoped that by now you might want to have a break, come back and see your family."

"Well, what if you and Father came here to visit me?" I asked. "I do have a spare bedroom, you know. And I could show you around town."

"It's not a terrible idea," she said. "But your father's back isn't what it used to be, and I worry that the long train ride on one of those uncomfortable seats might do more harm than good."

My heart sank, but I wasn't entirely surprised. "All right. Well you and Father discuss it. I would be happy to make something special for him for his birthday, you know."

"And you should reconsider as well," she said. "It will do you no good to stay holed up inside that shop, day in and day out."

"I know, Mother," I said.

There was a voice in the background of the phone call. "Oh, your sister just arrived, dear. I should let you go."

"Well, tell her and Mitchell that I said hello," I said. "And I love you all."

"Much love to you too, dear," Mother said, and then I heard the solid *click* of the call being disconnected.

I set the receiver back on the hook on the wall, sighing heavily.

I put the buttons aside, not wanting to deal with the tedious task any longer.

I then picked up the telephone once again and called Irene, who I knew would be a balm for my annoyance.

"When I moved away from home, I knew it was going to be difficult on them," I told her, returning to sorting the buttons, finding it almost therapeutic. "...But I never imagined it would turn into every conversation with her attempting to make me feel guilty about leaving in the first place."

"I'm sure she doesn't want you to feel guilty," Irene said. "More than anything, it's just her way of showing how much she cares."

"Well, she has a harsh way of showing it," I said rather cross. "And when I suggested that she and my father come and stay with me, she all but refused, claiming it would be too difficult for my father."

"That is a bit strange," Irene said. "I wonder how much of it is simply that she just misses your presence but doesn't know how to communicate it."

"I wondered that myself," I said. "When Roger died, she was against me taking my aunt's shop, especially since it was so far from home. She asked me over and over to change my mind, to stay in Plymouth."

"That would explain her bitterness," Irene said.

"Bitterness..." I said. "That's a very good word for it."

"Maybe you should consider going home for a break," Irene said. "I'm sure you could find someone to keep an eye on the shop for you. Perhaps that Sidney Mason who lives next door to you, hmm?"

My face flushed as I recognized the teasing tone in her voice. "Maybe I will, but not for some time. I still feel as if I am getting used to living here. And now that I was able to move past everything that happened with my aunt, and her death..." I said, trailing off. "I finally feel like I have peace here in this house, and it's almost as if I am starting over. I want to give myself time to adjust, and I worry that if I was to go home now, my mother would do everything in her power to change my mind."

"Are you concerned that you might listen to her, and move back?" Irene asked.

"No," I said. "But I am worried that it might make me utterly lose my patience with her and not want to speak with her ever again."

She and I laughed at that, and I started to feel much better about everything.

"Do you have the tea shop open?" I asked.

"Oh, yes," Irene said. "It's quiet today, though. Not surprising, since the weather is so pleasant. What about you? Are you opening your shop?"

"I must fill an order for Mrs. Trent, actually. Is she at the tea shop?" I asked.

"Yes, she's here," Irene said.

"Could you ask her to wait for me?" I asked. "I would be happy to deliver the parcel to her personally, if she would be willing to stay for another half hour or so."

"I'm sure she won't mind at all," Irene said warmly. "I'll go let her know."

"Thank you, Irene," I said.

"You're quite welcome, my dear," Irene said. "See you soon."

"See you," I said, and hung up the phone.

It only took me a few moments to collect Mrs. Trent's order, which consisted of a new spool of white thread, a dozen mother of pearl buttons, and a set of three new sewing needles for her machine. I bundled them all up in a small box, wrapped it in brown paper, and tied it with a piece of twine. I tucked the bud of a rose from the bush in my back garden under the twine, smiling, hoping that it might brighten her day, even just a little.

Everyone could do with something to make them smile...especially in these dark times.

I stepped out the front door, the scent of rain heavy in the air. The sky had begun to clear, however, the clouds already moving east in the sky, fractures of blue showing between tendrils of grey mist. Puddles scattered the streets, and the last of the raindrops to fall clung to the eaves of the houses across the street, just waiting for gravity to pull them down with the others.

I headed down the street, the package tucked beneath my arm. It was rather quiet, for a Monday afternoon. The shops weren't bustling like they usually were, especially not the grocer, which surprised me as I walked past. Their pulldown doors were rolled all the way up, and all the fresh produce was sitting in boxes, just waiting to be purchased by any of the families in town.

"That's strange..." I said, stopping just outside, peering in. I couldn't even see any of the workers back behind the counter. "Where is everyone?"

I kept walking, a tingle of apprehension making the small hairs on my neck stand up.

I turned onto Blackwood Street, where Irene's tea shop was located, and was startled by the sight of several dozen people gathered in the middle of the road.

Slowly, I approached, realizing they were all staring into the narrow alleyway between Mr. Englewood's house, and the butcher's shop, which were at the far end of the street, at the very edge of town. The green hills and the sheep fields belonging to the farmers outside of Brookminster lay beyond, deep green and lush after the rain.

I saw the butcher standing just outside his shop, talking with one of the police constables, wearing his usual blood-stained apron. I saw the end of his cleaver sticking out of the front pocket, and the expression on his face told me he was none too pleased about being interrupted in the middle of the day.

I also noticed a few of the grocer's helpers standing nearby, their heads bent together as they stared and pointed down through the alleyway.

Another familiar face revealed itself to me in the crowd. Nathanial Driscoll, Irene's husband, stood there with his arms folded across his chest, his brow furrowed, almost a head taller than anyone around him, and twice as wide.

I walked over to him, trying to see past the police and the other curious bystanders.

"Hello, Nathanial," I said as I got nearer.

"Oh, hello, Helen," Nathanial said, an effort at a smile

spreading across his face, although he was clearly distracted by something. "Nice to see you."

"You as well," I said.

"Were you on your way to see my wife?" he asked. "She's still over at the tea shop."

"I was, yes," I said, glancing over my shoulder at the shop I had passed to investigate the crowd. I showed him the package. "I actually was bringing this to Mrs. Trent."

"I see," he said.

"What's, uh...what's happening here?" I asked. "Though from the expression on everyone's faces, I'm not certain I want to know the answer."

Nathanial shook his head. "You may not, no," he said, seeming apprehensive.

I looked over in the direction of the alleyway, and saw a small building nestled between the others, one that I had never noticed before. Some sort of shack, or perhaps a shed for storage.

The police were stepping in and out of it, one with a camera, and others with gloves on their hands.

I noticed the police inspector, Sam Graves, standing off to the side, scratching notes on a pad of paper. The crease in his brow told me just how unhappy he was about the circumstances in which he found himself.

"Well, it must be something serious," I said, staring around at the grave expression on one particular police officer's face. "They all look as if they've seen a ghost."

"They've seen too many..." Nathanial said. He sighed heavily. "There was a body found in that shed back there. Apparently the shed belongs to Mr. Englewood, but as he was out of town visiting his sister in Brighton, he has no idea what happened."

My stomach twisted, and the fear snatched the breath right from my chest. "So how did someone discover it?" I asked.

"It seems the butcher was the one who discovered the body," Nathanial said. "Went out into his garden for some eggs from his coop, and from what I've heard, thought something smelled off…"

The bile churned in my stomach, and my face flushed.

"Naturally, he would be one to know when…well, when something was beginning to spoil. And I know Ronald. He does his very best to ensure that his meat never spoils, always tries to ensure that his customers are getting the very best of what he can offer."

Nathanial looked down at me, and became rather sheepish.

"I'm sorry, Helen. I don't want to disturb you with these troubling images," he said, scratching the back of his head nervously.

"No, it's quite all right," I said, staring past him at the shed between the two honey-colored buildings.

A body. Another death in this town.

I glanced over at Inspector Graves, who seemed absorbed in the notebook in his hands, as well as talking with the constable that had just walked up to him. He nodded solemnly, and when he lifted his head to look my direction, I swiftly sidestepped behind Nathanial.

I knew that Sam Graves would be rather displeased to find me near another body…especially just weeks after

Mrs. Martin's death. I did not need to give him any reason to suspect me of meddling.

Or worse yet, to think that I was some sort of curse upon this little village.

"It's quite a shame, really," Nathanial said, apparently entirely unaware of my inner musings or fears about Sam Graves. "With the war happening, you would think that a town like ours would be insulated from any further grief than what we already must endure. Is it so hard for people to try and keep peace?"

My heartbeat quickened. "Are you saying...this was a murder?" I asked.

He shrugged his shoulders. "That I'm not sure of. But it seems likely, given the place the body was found. If it was someone who had died of some sort of sudden illness, then they would have likely been discovered in their home, wouldn't they?" he asked.

"Wait, are you uncertain who the person was?" I asked.

"Well, yes," Nathanial said. "The police haven't let anyone near. And we know for sure it wasn't Mr. Englewood or any of his family; as I've said, they were all on holiday."

I furrowed my brow, fighting the nausea growing within me, as well as the curiosity that was making my mind whirl.

"It's probably best if we make our way from here, though," Nathanial said. "I'm certain we will hear about it all soon enough."

"Yes, I imagine we will," I said, somewhat distracted. "Nathanial, please tell your wife that I will be at the shop shortly. There's another errand I must take care of first that I suddenly remembered."

"Well, yes of course," Nathanial said with another one of his kind smiles. It was no wonder why Irene adored him so much. "We will see you soon. Oh, and would you care to stay for dinner this evening? Irene was hoping to make a cottage pie."

"That sounds wonderful," I said, the thought warming my heart a little, lessening some of the fear. I was so glad that I had found Irene and her family, who were quickly becoming like a family to me.

He smiled again and headed on his way back up the road, toward the tea shop.

I waited until he was far enough away before following after him, but only a short ways. I ducked between the next two buildings, between Mr. Englewood's home, and another home that had been sitting empty for some time.

Goose pimples spread across my arms as I walked through the cool, shadowy space between the houses.

What in the world are you doing? A voice somewhere in the back of my mind asked. *This is utterly crazy. Are you hoping to give yourself nightmares again, especially when they have just started to taper off?*

I was well aware that the voice was rational, and that I should listen to it.

What did I gain by getting a look at the body? What advantage would I have from glimpsing this person?

It was fear. Fear that it was someone I knew. Fear it was someone I cared for.

I had lost too many people, and while many in this

town were still new to me, I couldn't imagine having to lose any of them, my friends, the people who were helping me to feel at home.

Sidney Mason's face flickered across my vision, as well as that of sweet Mrs. Georgianna. I feared it might be any of my customers, or perhaps one of Irene's regular customers.

I reached the back of the houses, and found myself staring at the backs of two other houses that sat on the street parallel to Blackwood, with nothing more than some narrow patches of grass and another stone walking path separating them, a path that went all the way back to High Street. I glanced up and down the way, ensuring the coast was clear, and headed back south, back toward Mr. Englewood's opposite side yard where the shed stood.

As I reached the back of Mr. Englewood's house, I heard the low voices and the distinct *snap* of a camera from around the corner. The police were very close, and if I made one misstep, they would likely see me and chase me out of there.

And if Sam Graves caught me snooping around another body...

I gathered my courage, peering around the corner.

They were standing at the front of the shed, the door swung wide open. There was an unpleasant smell hanging in the air, and it took me a moment to realize what it must be.

I pulled a handkerchief from the inside of my sleeve and covered my nose with it, my eyes watering as I tried to keep what little breakfast I had eaten down.

The officers' backs were turned, and the door was

almost enough to obscure the space between the side of the shed and the side of the house.

I counted to three in my head...and dashed across the gap to the safety of the back of the shed.

My heart pounded in my chest as I pressed myself against the cool, weathered wood. I did my best to keep my breathing quiet as I looked around.

There was no one back here.

I looked to my right and saw a small, clouded window that looked as if it had not been cleaned in years.

Slowly, I moved toward it, careful to keep my ears tuned to the police, in case any of them came around to the back.

I peered in through the window, and was just able to make out a shape on the floor of the shed. At first, it looked like nothing more than a pile of old rags...but a moment later, I saw a hand, limp against the ground, stained with dark, dried blood.

My stomach clenched, and my mouth went dry.

My eyes moved through the rags, horror keeping my gaze pinned to every detail; the tear in the front of the jacket, dark blood staining all around it. The plain wedding ring on the bloody finger. The stillness and unmoving chest –

And then my gaze fell upon his face, and I gasped.

It was the Polish refugee.

4

I hadn't worn my black dress since Roger's funeral. It had hung in the back of my closet, still tucked away in its garment bag. I had hoped it would never see the light of day again. It wasn't as if the dress itself was anything special. It was rather simple; fell to the knees, with wide pleats and a clean hem, stitched with black. The collar was scalloped, white, and the only contrast to the whole outfit. The sleeves, long and straight, were unadorned. Two simple buttons, also black, finished the neckline.

My sister had picked it out. She said it suited me. But how could a dress suit a person whose heart had been broken? Was there a particular way that a woman who had just lost her husband should look? Was that what this dress said to those who saw me?

Memories washed over me as I pulled that dress back on. Every nerve in my body rejected it, cried at me to take it off. In my mind, I saw the graveside, the dirt damp and fresh, the mahogany casket lying down inside it...the last time I would ever see the final resting place of my Roger. I saw the dress hanging on the back of the closet door in my old bedroom at my parents house, my mother in tears as I told her that I was leaving Plymouth to start my life over, my voice so loud as I yelled in anger at her that my throat felt as if I was tearing it. I saw the dress folded up in my suitcase as I prepared to leave, as if I somehow cherished it like the other few things I had decided to bring with me to my new life...when in reality, I just couldn't imagine parting with something that I had worn to honor Roger and his life.

When I caught a glimpse of myself in the mirror in my bedroom, I had to remind myself that I was not, in fact, going to Roger's funeral. The pain, fresh again, roiled around inside me, the same heaviness weighing on my heart just as it had that day.

*That happened months ago...*I reminded myself. *Roger has been gone for almost six months. I am doing much better now. The days are easier. Sleep is easier. Yes, I miss him. All the time. But I am healing.*

I continued to remind myself of these truths as I finished getting dressed, pinned my hair up in a jeweled barrette that Roger had given me before we were married, and added some simple, black heels. I found a small enough purse to tuck my handkerchief and my lipstick inside before leaving the house.

The wind had picked up overnight, causing me to clutch at my skirt to prevent it from blowing up at all as I walked.

The church, beautiful in its ancient stone, stood atop the hill nearer the center of town, its steeple stretching high into the sky, taller than any of the trees around it. Bells began to chime just as the hour of noon arrived, echoing all through Brookminster.

I received some strange looks as I went, from acquaintances as well as others. One such person was the butcher's wife, Annie. She was busy minding her young son and daughter, yet she gave me a kind smile as I drew nearer to them. "Good afternoon, Helen," she said, her eyes immediately dipping down toward my somber appearance. "My goodness, you look as if you might be headed to a funeral...is everything all right?"

"Oh, well, that is precisely where I am going," I said.

Annie seemed stunned. "Who was it that passed away?" she asked. "Is it anyone I know?"

I glanced down at her children, the boy sticking his tongue out at his older sister when neither she nor her mother were watching, and chose my words carefully, so as not to upset young ears. "It was that poor refugee that your husband – " I began, but both pairs of little eyes darted up toward me at the mention of their father.

"Good heavens," Annie said, her eyes widening. "I had no idea they were having a service for him..."

"Yes," I said. "I imagine it will be rather small, perhaps not well attended. I don't think he knew anyone in town."

"Why are you going?" Annie asked, her brow wrinkling. "Did you know him?"

I shook my head. "I met him very briefly a few days ago. He was looking for someone, and wanted help. My neighbor, Sidney Mason, took him down to the police station, but something tells me he was never able to find who he was looking for."

"How sad," Annie said, concern clouding her pretty, delicate features. She was a dainty woman to be married to a butcher. "I will head home at once and tell Ronald, but I am certain he won't be able to leave the shop on such short notice..."

"It's quite all right," I said, shaking my head. "There's no need to explain that to me. Besides, it isn't as if he will know who was able to come or not..."

Annie gave me a sad, yet understanding look.

"Well...regardless, it was good to see you, Helen. Perhaps we should have tea at Irene's soon?" she asked.

"I would like that," I said.

"Very good," Annie said. "I'll be seeing you!"

"You as well," I said, and continued on down the road toward the church.

Concern began to creep up within me. I had thought for certain that the butcher would have attended the funeral, given he had been the one to find the poor man...

I had heard about the funeral that Sunday during church, even if Mr. James had only mentioned it briefly. I had imagined that a great deal many more would have heard, as the news about his death had spread across town like wildfire. Before the day was through on the morning he had been found, everyone knew what had happened. Many suspected murder, given the strange location of the body, but some were convinced that he had wandered in there in the middle of a drunken stupor and had accidentally shot himself, although no weapon had been found in the shed.

All of this I had heard through secondhand sources, mostly the wives of the police officers, or those who were too nosy for their own good. Irene, however, working at the tea shop, had heard more details about it than anyone.

She and Nathanial were unable to attend the funeral due to their shop being open, and Nathanial being away on business in London to retrieve a fresh supply of tea from the shipyards. They had a special supplier that liked to be paid in person.

"But come right here afterward, all right?" Irene urged me as we had left church together two days before. "I'll make sure to brew you up some fresh tea to soothe that tired, sad soul you'll be bringing back with you."

If I was honest with myself, that was all that was helping me to get through, knowing that I could much more easily move past this funeral than I had Roger's, and that I could be with a friend and relax later.

When I reached the doors of the church, however, my sadness returned as I stared into a very empty sanctuary.

My footsteps echoed off the vaulted ceiling overhead, the pale light of the day filtering in through the stained glass windows depicting different stories of the Bible; David and Goliath, Joseph and his brothers, Abraham and his son Isaac...

A simple table was set up just before the altar. A bouquet of flowers, small and simple, sat upon it. Two candles burned on either side of it.

"Ah, Mrs. Lightholder. I'm surprised to see you here."

I looked around and saw the vicar, Mr. James, stepping out of his office, off to the side of the sanctuary.

He was a rather handsome man, thin and lean, with dark hair that was greying around his temples. Thin faced and narrow jawed, he had the features of a man who spent a great deal of time reading, and not nearly enough caring for himself. He wore tortoise shell spectacles that complimented the green of his eyes, and a long dark robe.

"Did I...am I here at the wrong time?" I asked, looking around.

"For the funeral?" Mr. James asked, walking toward me. He adjusted his glasses, shaking his head. "No, I'm afraid not. To be quite honest, I was rather certain that no one would be showing up. He was a complete stranger to everyone in town, and from what I have heard, was a bit troublesome to others." He sighed, pursing his lips thoughtfully. "Even so, I expected there would be some that might come to pay their respects out of kindness..."

His brow furrowed as he looked at me.

"Why did you decide to come?" he asked, and I fell into step beside him as he started toward the front of the church.

"Well..." I said. "Sidney Mason and I met the man some time ago, and...I don't know. He was looking for someone, seemed almost desperate. And with this war going on, haven't we all lost someone?" I trailed off. "I'm sorry, I suppose I just hoped he would have been able to find whoever he was looking for, and something tells me he did not..."

Mr. James nodded his head. "Well, it was very kind of you to come. It certainly does not matter who we are, or where we have come from. God made us all, and He cares about each one of us. This refugee from Germany was no different, for God loves them as well."

"I believe he was from Poland," I said.

"Really?" Mr. James said. "There were a great many people who told me he was German...well, no matter. It's tragic that he lost his life here, and I certainly wish it had turned out differently for him."

"As do I..." I said.

He took a deep breath, glancing back at the doors to the sanctuary. "I have a feeling we aren't going to have many more guests. Perhaps we should get started?"

"Yes, I think so," I said.

I took a seat in the front pew, and instead of speaking from a distance, Mr. James came around to stand beside the table, his Bible lying open in his hands.

His message was short. Neither of us knew the man's name, nor anything about him apart from what I had gleaned the day I had met him.

"The book of Ezekiel says, *For I have no pleasure in the death of anyone, declares the Lord God*. Death is a result of the fall of man, and something not meant to be endured by men. Yet, as we live in a fallen world, with our fallen natures, we must endure the pain and suffering that loss and death brings us. However...hope is not lost. Second Corinthians says; *So we are always of good courage. We know that while we are at home in the body we are away from the Lord, for we walk by faith, not by sight. Yes, we are of good courage, and we would rather be away from the body and at home with the Lord*."

Shortly after his message, we made our way out to the cemetery behind the church. The wind still raced through the trees, making the branches flutter and sway. I wished I'd brought a sweater with me, as the air was quite a bit cooler than I remembered.

We walked all the way to the back of the cemetery, to a corner of the churchyard that overlooked the valley and all its beautiful rolling hills.

I saw the casket, already settled into the dirt. It was a small area, nestled between a tree and some rose bushes.

"This was a plot that was never chosen by families in the town," Mr. James said as we stood in front of the open grave. "No one wished to be buried alone, regardless of how beautiful this place is."

Beautiful it certainly was. And peaceful.

"We can be hopeful for our own deaths," Mr. James said, staring down at the polished casket. "Because our Savior walked out of his own grave, having risen three days after he had been killed by those who hated him. We can have hope for our friend, then, knowing that he has met the Lord, face to face."

I noticed the headstone was unmarked.

Mr. James must have noticed my gaze fixed on the headstone. "It makes me sad, as well, but I didn't want to disgrace him by putting a name upon it that was not his own. I had no idea of his age, either, and it seemed rather morose to put nothing more than the date of his death upon the stone. I thought it might be best just to leave it blank, even though I know it will create many questions from others."

"I understand," I said, though I thought it was sad. The only people who would know that he was here would be Mr. James and I, and soon, everyone in our little village of Brookminster would surely forget he had ever been here in the first place.

"Do you know how he died?" I asked, looking up at the vicar.

Mr. James exhaled out of his nose, his gaze somewhat distant. "No," he said. "And to be honest, it wasn't important for me to do my duties. All I knew was that I needed to prepare a place for him to be buried, so that's what I did."

"Well...thank you, Mr. James," I said. "For being so kind."

"It was no trouble at all," he said. "I just worry now about his family, if he had any...they'll never know what happened to him. And as we didn't know his name, they'll never be able to find him, either. I wonder if he would have been buried alongside his wife, or his parents, if he had stayed back wherever he came from..."

That was something I had not considered. It was terribly sad to think of his living family, wondering where in the world he had ended up. And not for the first time, I wondered again who, exactly, it was that he had been looking for.

"Thank you again for coming," Mr. James said, closing his Bible and tucking it beneath his arm. "It was a very gracious thing to do."

"It was no trouble," I said with a smile.

I departed as a worker arrived, picked up a shovel that had been laid aside, and begun to fill in the grave. The methodic sound of the *chink* of the dirt in the ground followed the tumbling *shoosh* of soil as it slid off the shovel and into the grave. Every few scoops, I heard the dirt banging against the wooden coffin, and my stomach clenched.

That poor man was inside, never to see the light of day ever again...

At least, not on this earth.

My heart ached for him. I ached for what could have been for him. I wondered how his life could have come to such a sudden, tragic end.

Then I wondered if anyone in town might have learned more about him. Maybe even discovered his name.

That...and I couldn't stop thinking about Nathanial's assumption that the poor refugee had likely been murdered.

Who would have done such a thing? And to a complete stranger?

These were certainly dangerous times we were living in, but to murder someone –

"You of all people, huh?"

I nearly jumped out of my skin.

I wheeled around and found Inspector Graves, leaning up against the trunk of one of the ancient trees in the churchyard. His gaze was fixed on the distant grave, where Mr. James lingered while the worker diligently filled in the hole around the casket that was just visible in the earth.

Sam Graves' foot was propped up on the tree behind him, and his arms were folded in front of himself.

"Oh, Inspector Graves..." I said. "I didn't know you were here."

He shifted his gaze to me, his blue eyes piercing

beneath his dark lashes.

I swallowed hard, both unsettled and strangely entranced by his intense stare.

"First I find you outside the shop of Sandra Martin, who was attempting to kill you, and now here I find you at the graveside of a stranger, who had no family, no name..." He shifted his shoulders, leaning down toward me. "Are you going to tell me that you knew this man somehow? Or perhaps were related to him?"

"N – no," I said, taking a hesitant step back. His gaze was quelling, making me feel like a schoolgirl caught misbehaving. "I met him while he was alive, and – "

"And what?" he asked.

I clutched the purse in my hands, and attempted to stand a bit straighter. "Inspector Graves, I don't know what you are implying, but I was simply attending this poor man's funeral. As you can see, there wasn't anyone else here. At least it wasn't quite so lonely."

"Hmph..." he said. "I was here, too."

"Yes, you were," I said.

A brief moment of silence passed between us, with nothing but the wind to fill the space.

"I shouldn't have to say this..." he said, his eyes narrowing. "But it may not be the wisest idea to get too involved with anything that has to do with this man."

My brow wrinkled. "What does that mean?"

His gaze hardened. "You now have a history of meddling where you shouldn't, and getting yourself into trouble."

"Are you implying I had something to do with his death?" I asked, shocked.

He shook his head. "No. You aren't a killer. That much is obvious. But you seem to be one of those people that tragedy likes to hang around..."

My heart sank at his words. Tragedy followed me around? "That's an unkind thing to say to someone..." I said.

He shrugged. "That doesn't mean it isn't true."

"So you're saying that someone did kill the poor refugee?" I asked.

His face suddenly went blank. "All I am saying is that you need to keep your distance. As kind as it was for you to come to the funeral, this is where your influence should stop. For your safety."

I folded my arms, staring at him coolly. "Even though I was the one who figured out that Sandra Martin murdered my aunt?"

"That was different," Sam said. "You had access to information that no one did...which you should have brought to me in the first place so that you never would have been in danger from her."

My face flushed, and I looked down. He was right about that, I supposed.

"Just...be wise, all right? Don't let your curiosity get the better of you," he said. "You know what they say, right? What happened to the cat when it got too curious?"

Throat growing tight, I glanced over my shoulder. Mr. James was still watching the man with the shovel as he filled the grave.

"I understand," I said, the little hairs on the back of my neck standing up. "Loud and clear."

5

"I'm really sorry I didn't get to go to that funeral yesterday," Sidney said as he leaned against the counter in my kitchen, sipping the tea I had just made for him. "If I had been in town, I certainly would have."

"It's all right," I said, taking a seat at the table and picking up my own cup.

He breathed in deeply, his nose poised over his cup. "There's always something so comforting about tea, isn't there?" he asked.

"I couldn't agree more," I said. "Even when it's near boiling outside, I still can't pass up having a few cups throughout the day."

He let out an appreciative hum as he lowered his cup, smiling.

"Were you out doing another job?" I asked.

"Yes," he said, setting his teacup down and picking up his hammer once again. "Out at one of the farms outside the village. The farmer's wife ran into me in town the other day, and we started talking. She said her sink had started to leak, and she and her husband couldn't figure out how or why. So I offered to come and work on it for them."

"That was awfully kind of you," I said. "Was it a long way outside of town?"

"Not really, no," he said. "Mr. Trent was kind enough to take me in his car. The one I recently acquired still needs some tuning up. Should be ready in a week or two, though."

I thought of the pale blue number sitting in his driveway, somewhat rusty and certainly in need of care. But as with many things about Sidney, the car was just another mystery.

He picked up another trimmed board of wood, and opened up the upper cabinet door that had broken almost a week before. The hinges had suddenly come lose, and it wouldn't screw back into the wood.

"I'm sorry I keep calling you about things breaking in this house," I said, looking around. "When I first moved in, everything seemed to be in good condition. The more I live here, though, the more I see how dated and tired everything is."

"It happens in these older houses," Sidney said, holding the board up to the inside of the cabinet, and drawing a line across the wood to measure it. "For instance, in my own kitchen, I have already replaced three of the bottom cabinets, all of the shelves in the top cabinets, and have started to cut the boards I will need for a new counter. The stone one that is there now is chipped and cracked, and really has no place in a kitchen."

"Goodness, I had no idea it was so bad," I said.

He set down the board and tucked the pen behind his ear, something I had seen him do several times now unconsciously. "It really isn't. I am just not all that fond of the idea of my kitchen cabinets falling apart when I least expect it."

I glanced up at the clock beside the ice box, the pendulum beneath it swinging rhythmically like always. "Oh, good heavens," I said, getting to my feet. "I wasn't aware that it was so late."

Sidney looked up, eyes falling on the clock. "Nor I. I'm sorry for distracting you."

"No, it's quite all right," I said. "There are some deliveries that I must make in town. Will you be all right if I leave you here alone for a bit to finish up?"

"That's perfectly fine," he said. "If you leave me a key, then I should be able to get it all done for you in no time."

"That I can do," I said. "I'll leave it right here on the table. When you're done, feel free to set it on the soil in that green flowerpot near the door."

"Will do," he said, picking up his teacup once again, smiling at me over the rim.

"Thank you, Sidney," I said with a wave as I hurried down the stairs to the shop.

I found the orders, already filled earlier that day when the shop had been open, and picked them up before hurrying toward the door. I had three orders to deliver, one rather urgent.

My first stop was to Mrs. Georgianna. She was my most pressing delivery, so I stopped there first.

"Oh, thank goodness," she said when she answered the door and saw me with the package. She grinned at me and paid me well, taking the box with bright eyes and a girlish giggle for someone in her seventies. "I was hoping these would be ready tonight. My husband and I are heading to a military dinner, and I was hoping to fix up the buttons on his uniform before we went."

"Well, I'm happy to be of service," I said.

"Have you considered taking up what Mrs. Martin was doing at her shop?" Mrs. Georgianna asked. "You know, selling clothing as well as what you already do?"

"I have," I said. "I just wasn't sure if someone else in her family might end up picking up her shop just like I did with my aunt's."

Mrs. Georgianna shook her head. "I would be amazed if anyone did, dear. I would think on it, if I were you. There are many people in this village who would be happy to have that sort of service available once again, regardless of the rations on clothing and the like. Not to mention it would surely give you a greater and perhaps even steadier source of income..."

It was certainly something to consider, I realized as I wandered over toward Irene's tea shop. She had ordered some lace to refinish some of her tablecloths. Would it be wise to do exactly as Mrs. Martin had feared in the beginning, and take over her business completely?

"I think it's a fine idea," Irene said when I broached the subject with her a short time later. "Mrs. Martin certainly was a bitter woman and was protective of her store, but that was rooted in greed and jealousy. I know there would be many in town who would support your decision, and I would certainly be among that number."

I nodded, my thoughts chasing themselves around in my mind, all of the positives and negatives that could come out of it.

"I have one more delivery to make," I said, glancing down at the note I'd written for myself. "It's for Mr. Newton, but I don't have any idea where I might find him. He came by the shop a few days ago, but I forgot to get his address."

"That's not a problem," Irene said, untying her apron and hanging it on the hook beside the door in the kitchen. "He's the cook down at The Honey and Rose."

"The inn?" I asked. "I've never been there."

"Well, why don't I go with you?" she asked, smiling at me. "I'm sure Michael will be happy to tag along as well. Henry Newton is one of his closest friends."

"That sounds wonderful," I said.

"I'll just fetch him from upstairs," she said. "He'll be glad for a break from his schoolwork, I'm sure of it."

Grateful he was. A few minutes later, I laughed as we watched him skip down the road ahead of us, cheering excitedly as he ran.

Irene just smiled and shook her head. "It's so easy to make them happy when they're that young," she said. "You'll see one day, I'm sure."

I smiled. "I would certainly like to."

Irene gave me a rather sly look. "And how are things going with that Sidney Mason?" she asked.

I gaped at her, astonished. "Oh, Irene, you know very well that – "

"He's a handsome young man, and you are a very pretty young woman?" she asked, a twinkle in her grey eyes. "Oh, come now, I am only teasing. But even still…"

Glad that we had arrived at the inn, I was able to quickly move the subject of conversation away from Sidney.

The Honey and Rose was a pretty building on the corner of High Street and Magnolia Avenue, which sat right in the heart of town. It was at the bottom of one of the low hills, but had a wonderful view of the river that snaked around the town itself. A bridge crossed over, giving access to the rest of Brookminster.

The building itself was made of the same warm, honey-toned stones as the other houses. It was two stories tall, with every wall plastered with windows and slightly rickety, old shutters. A worn, wooden sign hung above the lead-pane windowed door, swinging in the gentle after-noon breeze.

Michael was already there, pulling the door open and hurrying inside.

"Michael, wait," Irene called. She shook her head when he disappeared without even a glance in her direc-tion. "Honestly, I swear sometimes that he has lost the ability to hear my voice."

We followed after him, stepping inside the inn.

The first thing I noticed was the heavy scent of ale and firewood, as well as polished floors, which gleamed beneath our feet. Every table was neatly and evenly arranged, and the chairs were spaced equally apart from one another.

There were even roses in small bud vases on each table.

The bar along the back wall ran all the way from one side to the other, and barstools ran along in front of it, all equally spaced once again.

There wasn't a thing out of place. There were no dirty tankards or plates on the tables, and not a crumb to be seen on the floor.

"This might be the cleanest inn I have ever been in," I said, staring around in amazement.

"Mrs. Diggory, the innkeeper's wife, is a very meticulous woman," Irene said with a smile. "She would no more allow her husband to wreck this place than she would let him feed their own child to the Loch Ness monster."

That much was clear.

There was a rather surly looking man up behind the counter, wiping down the polished wooden surface with a clean rag. The way he polished that one spot, it was as if it had personally wronged him in some way.

"Good afternoon, Mr. Diggory," Irene said kindly as we walked toward the bar. "How are you doing?"

The man looked up, and immediately I sensed Irene's question was the wrong one. His face seemed gaunt, his eyes sunken in. The irises, deep blue, were rimmed in red veins as if he hadn't slept in weeks.

"What'll it be?" he asked, tossing the rag onto the counter rather forcefully.

Irene seemed surprised, too. "Oh, nothing for us.

Helen here just needed to make a quick delivery to Mr. Newton. Is he here?"

"Down in the kitchens," Mr. Diggory said sourly, snatching up the cloth once again and aggressively going after the same already pristine spot on the counter.

"Right," Irene said, watching him warily. "We'll be out of your way shortly."

I followed her back to a wooden door that was the same material as the rest of the warm wood paneling around the rest of the room. She pulled it open and we stepped inside.

A wooden stairwell surrounded by rough, stone walls met us, and welcomed us downward. Lanterns hung in regular intervals all the way down.

The bottom floor of the inn was like stepping into a medieval building. The walls were all formed from stone, with an arched ceiling that was so low I could reach up and brush my hands against it. Open doorways lead off the hall, which was also made of stone that had been worn smooth by years of footsteps passing over it.

It smelled of rosemary and thyme as we wandered down the hall, and steam hovered near the ceiling, billowing out of one of the doorways at the end of the short hall.

We stepped inside a kitchen that was three times the size of my own, and was the exact opposite of the inn's tidy dining room upstairs.

Pots were stacked along the far wall, and piled high in the sink, all stained with sauces and residue. Bowls were coated with flour, and pans with crusted bits of pies and roasts.

There was a large counter in the center of the room, and every bit of its surface was covered in herbs and foods that were in the middle of being prepared. Knives and bowls were waiting for more ingredients, already partially filled with chopped meats, or boiled potatoes, or stewed tomatoes.

The stove was covered in pots that were simmering, steaming, or boiling over. Everything seemed chaotic, and there was only one man at the helm, working to keep it all under control.

"Well, hello there, Mrs. Driscoll," said the round-faced man standing at the stove. He wheeled around, the front of his apron splattered with a bright red tomato sauce, and flecks of spattered oil. He wielded a spatula, which dripped its porridge-like mixture onto the floor beneath him, unnoticed entirely by the man.

"Hello, Mr. Newton," Irene said.

"Ah, and I see you've come with Mrs. Lightholder," Mr. Newton said, grinning at me. "It's wonderful to see you."

"It's a pleasure to see you as well, sir," I said. "I brought your order for you."

"Oh, splendid, splendid," he said, setting the spatula down beside a raw slab of beef that was apparently waiting to be seasoned and cooked. "How fortunate it is for me that you brought these when you did. My wife will be so pleased."

I passed him the box of silks that he had chosen for his wife.

"These are wonderful," he said. "Such fine silks. My wife intends to make one of these into a tie for me."

"That does sound nice," Irene said. She looked around. "I see you are hard at work, as usual."

"Oh, yes, of course," he said. "The Diggorys are expecting a large group of guests this evening. Apparently the family of Elizabeth Warner is coming in for their wedding."

"Oh, is that this weekend?" Irene asked. "Thank you for reminding me. I shall have to find a suitable gift, as I'm sure Nathanial will want to go."

Then her gaze hardened slightly, and she folded her arms.

"George...is everything all right with Mr. Diggory?" Irene asked. "He seemed perturbed when we spoke with him."

Mr. Newton's face fell, all traces of his smile disappearing. "Oh, yes...that," he said. He sighed, shaking his head as he moved from the stove to one of the bowls of chopped veggies, grabbing a large salt grinder and twisting the freshly ground flakes into the bowl. "It's dreadful news, really...straight from London, it was." He looked up, his eyes full of sadness. "It seems their boy's plane was shot down by the Luftwaffe recently."

"Their son was in the Royal Air Force?" I asked, my stomach twisting into knots. I was all too familiar with the danger that could come without warning from the skies these days...as the German airplanes had been the ones to drop the bombs over London when Roger was killed... It was boys like this one Mr. Newton spoke of who protected the rest of us or died trying to.

"Yes," Mr. Newton said with a fervent nod. "It just

happened about two weeks ago. I suppose they haven't told many people in town, yet."

"I heard about the downed planes over London," Irene said. She shook her head solemnly. "Oh, poor Nancy...she and Jonathon must be devastated."

"They certainly are..." Mr. Newton said. "I only had a brief moment to talk with them this morning about it, but Jonathon is taking it a great deal harder than his wife is. He believes it is his fault, through and through."

"How could it be, though?" Irene asked. "It isn't as if he was the one who sent their son to enlist, right?"

Mr. Newton gave her a pointed look.

"He...did?" Irene asked, laying a hand over her heart. "Oh, good heavens..."

"He urged the boy to become an RAF pilot, told him to make his family proud," he said.

"How could he have known this would happen?" I asked. "It's a terrible idea for him to blame himself the way he is..."

"I couldn't agree more, but I don't think that's something he will be able to hear for some time yet..." Mr. Newton said. "He is going to need time to heal. They both are."

We said goodbye to Mr. Newton shortly after that, making our way back upstairs into the inn.

Some of the guests that Mr. Newton had spoken of seemed to have arrived, and were sitting at the bar, chatting with one another while Mr. Diggory served them drinks.

"...At least it's better than that blasted German beggar skulking around here..." I heard Mr. Diggory say, the bitterness coating his every word. His nose wrinkled, and the hand holding the glass began to tremble, clattering against the surface of the bar.

I stopped near the door, and stared across the room at him.

The German beggar? He couldn't mean –

"That fool came around here and had the audacity to ask me for food! And shelter! For free! What did he think I was, some sort of sympathizer?" Mr. Diggory exclaimed, his gaze distant, his cheeks splotchy and red.

Some of the guests were giving each other nervous looks, others staring fixedly at Mr. Diggory.

It made me wonder how this whole conversation had started in the first place.

I swallowed hard. If he was talking about the refugee that had just been killed four days ago, then –

"What's the matter?" Irene asked.

My eyes stayed fixed on Mr. Diggory. "It's Mr. Diggory, he's – "

"He won't be bothering me anymore, no sir. No he will not. He's as dead as can be now. Good riddance, if you ask me. One less German in this world is – "

I went to step forward toward the bar, but Irene laid her hand on my shoulder.

"What is it?" I asked.

Irene shook her head. "I don't think it's wise to confront him," she said in a low voice.

"But he thinks that poor refugee was German," I said. "We both know he wasn't. What good is there in him hating a man for reasons that aren't even true?"

"It won't do any good," Irene said. "All he will think is that you are trying to protect him."

"You don't think he would believe me?" I asked.

"He wouldn't want to believe you right now," she said. "Think about it, Helen. The man just lost his son...it will be a long time before he will be able to think rationally about anything that has to do with his son's death. The military, the war, the enemy...it won't matter."

My heart ached at hearing the Polish man's life being so despised by this man, but in a way, I understood what Irene was trying to say.

"You're right," I said. "I suppose it doesn't really matter now anyways, does it, since he's dead..."

Irene led me from the inn, my mind whirling.

I had known that many in the village had thought the refugee was a German, and for the first time, I questioned Sidney's initial understanding of the man as well. What if he was simply pretending to speak Polish? What if he was, in fact, someone from the German military who was undercover? Maybe a German pilot who'd been shot down over English soil and found himself stranded?

These ideas were troubling, but it helped me to understand why Mr. Diggory might have been as upset as he was.

"It's a shame that Mr. Diggory was so angry with that poor beggar," Irene said. "Especially since the police haven't yet found a killer."

My stomach flipped, and I stared up at her. "You don't think...Mr. Diggory?"

Her brow creased. "I cannot imagine it..." she said. "I have known Mr. and Mrs. Diggory for many, many years.

Nancy since we were children. Yet I have never experi-
enced the anguish of losing a child. Would the pain of it
drive someone to such extreme measures?"

The thought was truly a troubling one, and neither of
us could seem to talk the other out of it. We could not
know for certain, yet at the same time, and equally as
frightening, we could imagine why someone would lash
out like that.

"Well, I'm sure it won't be long before Mr. Diggory's
dislike of anyone of German descent reaches those who
might have influence in the situation," Irene said. "We
won't have to worry."

I hoped she was right. For the time being, the idea of
someone being pushed so far to the breaking point that
they would ever consider harming another person in
such a manner...

Grief and sorrow were dark emotions, ones that I was
far too familiar with. I knew how horrible those first
weeks could be...how desperate, how hopeless.

Worry prevented me from feeling any peace for the
rest of the day.

6

The next morning, things seemed less hopeless to me. Taking time to rationally consider the situation, I realized it was less likely that Mr. Diggory had killed the beggar than I had originally thought. Irene knew him to be a good man, and he was a respected member of the community.

That, and if he had been the one to kill the beggar, then why would he have been so brashly talking about his death in the inn the way he had been? Wouldn't that just be asking for unwanted attention?

Even still, the memory of Irene's uncertainty kept popping up in my thoughts as I tended to customers and filled orders the next day. My thoughts were never far from the poor refugee, once again.

I closed the shop at three, just like I did every day. I was just locking the door when there was a knock upon it.

I saw Irene's face smiling in at me from the window in the door.

"Oh, hello, Irene," I said, opening it back up again. "I wasn't expecting to see you today. Please, come in. I can make us some tea."

"That's quite all right, dear," Irene said. "I was coming by to ask if you might be available this evening."

"Yes, as far as I'm aware," I said. I noticed that her arms were laden with packages and bags. "Can I help you with anything?"

She tipped a few boxes and one of the bags into my arms, sighing. I noticed sweat glistening near her hairline. "I was wondering if you would be interested in going with me to the Evermore estate this evening."

"Evermore – " I said, and then Mrs. Trent's story at the tea shop came back to me. "Oh, is that the place that was converted into a hospital?"

"The very same," Irene said, glancing down at the packages. "These are all meant to be for the soldiers, and some for the staff. It's a variety of items I've collected from those generous enough to donate necessities. Things like bandages, food, and blankets."

"Oh, what a wonderful idea," I said, a warm glow of generosity spreading through me. "I might have some things to contribute, as well."

"That's good news," Irene said.

"Give me just a moment, I know exactly what to bring," I said. I hurried back inside and ran upstairs.

I went to the attic and found a box of Aunt Vivian's blankets that I knew I would never use myself. I had washed them and stored them away, hoping to maybe find a use for the fabric. This, I knew, was a much better cause.

"Are we ready?" Irene asked, jostling the packages she held.

"Yes," I said, doing my best to hold the ones I had. "But...are we walking all the way there?" I asked.

Irene laughed. "No, dear. We're just walking back to the house. Nathanial offered to drive us there."

"Oh, good," I said, my arms already sagging under the weight of the packages and bags.

THE EVERMORE ESTATE was only a few miles outside of Brookminster. It was away from the bustle of the village, but as we pulled into the winding drive that snaked up one of the rolling hills, I could see the village in the distance.

"It looks like a toy set," I said. "Surrounded by all those fields."

Irene laughed. "It certainly is much smaller when you aren't in the middle of it, isn't it?" she asked.

The house was at the very top of the hill, pressed up against a small, forested stretch of land. It was a stunning property, a true relic of our country's heritage. The house was made of the same pale stone that my house was, yet where my home was nothing more than a simple cottage, this house was a manor fit for nobility.

Ivy climbed the walls, circling around the many windows on the front side of the house. The roof, adorned with three large dormers, gave the house its grand character. Two chimneys stretched high into the sky, smoke billowing upward into the cloudy early evening expanse. The front door was nestled in an outcropping of its own, with a peaked roof and a rounded staircase leading up to it.

"I don't know if I have ever seen such a magnificent place..." I said as Nathanial pulled the car up right out front. "You said a lord lives here?"

"Yes, Lord Evermore," Nathanial said. "The house itself is called Northernwood Hall, but it has been many years since it was referred to by that name."

"Yes, perhaps when Queen Victoria was around," Irene said. "The Evermores have lived here for some time now, several generations I believe."

I could only stare out the window, up at the marvelous home. I wondered how people like the Evermores dealt with times of war. Would all members of the upper classes step up the same way the Evermores had, and offer up their homes to those in need?

Upper class or not, I cannot think of many who would be willing to do this at all, I mused.

"Shall I help you ladies get these things inside?" Nathanial asked.

"That sounds good," Irene said. She glanced back at me in the rear seat. "How do you feel about staying for a little while, and meeting with some of the soldiers that are here?"

Nervousness was my first response, but I swiftly quelled it. "I think that's a great idea," I said. "It would be a chance to thank them for their service to our country."

"I will make sure you don't have to see any gruesome wounds or anything," Irene said with a smile. "Sometimes these poor fellows just want someone they can talk to about ordinary things. If they ask you all about your life, don't be too surprised. It allows them to leave their own thoughts behind for a little while."

I had never thought of that, but even as she said it, it made perfect sense.

We were greeted at the front door by a smiling man with snow white hair. He was dressed in a fine suit.

"Good evening," the man said with a smile. "I am Mr. Rogers. You are Mr. and Mrs. Driscoll, yes?" he asked.

"Yes," Mr. Driscoll said, swiveling to the side so that he could see the man behind the stack of boxes he was carrying. "That's us. And we brought along a friend, as well."

The man looked to me, smiled, and bowed his head. "Lord Evermore will be pleased with your willingness to sacrifice an evening of your time to deliver some goods to these poor gentlemen here. Please, allow me to show you the way."

We followed him through a grand foyer, with marble floors, gold gilded mirrors on the wall, and wallpaper that very well might have been original to the estate.

It was quite a shock, though, to see so many things out of place in the house. In the halls, for instance, extra beds and stretchers were lined up against one wall. Medical kits were stacked beside doorways. Nurses strolled in and out of rooms, their white uniforms pristine. These sights clearly did not belong in a home like this.

The air smelled sterile, and everything seemed eerily still. Even with the sconces aglow along the walls, and the chandeliers overhead gleaming bright, a heaviness hung in the air as we made our way toward the back of the estate.

"Right this way," Mr. Rogers said, gesturing into a doorway down a side hall.

It was a parlor of some sort, with shelves from floor to ceiling filled with books. The lovely, antique furniture had been haphazardly pushed up against the walls, some covered in white cloths to protect them.

In the middle of the room were tables laden with packages similar to the ones we had brought, and nurses who were unpacking and sorting through them.

One nurse looked up upon our entry, her face breaking into a grin. "Irene!" she exclaimed, hurrying around the tables, pulling the gloves she wore from her fingers.

She threw her arms around Irene's neck, standing almost a head shorter than her, and looking very slender compared to Irene's wide hips and shoulders.

"Hello, May," Irene said. She looked over at me, her arm around the woman's shoulders. "Helen, this is my cousin May. May, this is a friend of mine from the village."

"Nice to meet you," May said, hurrying to me and snatching my hand, her eyes, grey just like her cousin's, wide with excitement. Her pretty, auburn hair was tied up in a knot behind her head, and she wore a plain, white nurse's bonnet on top of her head. "I've heard a great deal about you from Irene!"

"It's nice to meet you as well," I said, smiling at her as she shook my hand.

May spun around, her quickness reminding me of a

rabbit's. "Are those all the supplies you managed to acquire?" she asked, her eyes widening.

"Yes," Nathanial said, setting the stack of boxes down. "I hope it will be enough."

"Enough?" May said, zipping around to the stack of boxes, delight evident on her face. "This is wonderful! You have both, as always, gone far above and beyond anything we could have imagined."

Irene and I set down the things we were carrying, as well.

"I managed to secure more blankets," Irene said. "Helen brought some, as well."

"That's wonderful," May said. "Even though it's the middle of summer, this cavernous house can be rather cool in the evenings. This was very kind, thank you."

"We also managed to bring more food," Nathanial said. "We were careful the last few weeks and saved some of our rationings."

May and I both looked over at Nathanial, May with adoration, and me with shock. They had stretched their own food allowance so that they might help these men in need?

It made me feel guilty at once for not having thought of it myself.

"You both are far too kind," May said. "You certainly have brought us enough to keep us busy. In the meantime, would you like to come and sit with some of the soldiers while we prepare their evening meal for them?"

She led us back through the door into the hall, and continued on toward the front door. For a moment, I thought we might be heading outside. My mind filled with images of long, white tents outside, packed to the brim with soldiers lying in cots. Those thoughts were dispelled, though, as we turned down another hall where voices and coughing and some groans of pain could be heard.

She took the first right into another room that was, at first, rather difficult to place. There was a large, stone fire-place at one end, which was roaring and bright, and a polished, wooden floor. There was no furniture, aside from a dozen or so beds that were spread across the room. Perhaps it was a dining hall? Or another parlor?

My eyes didn't linger long on the room as a whole, though. Instead, they fell upon the men stretched out in the beds, tucked beneath white sheets, with white bandages covering their hands, parts of their arms, or even their heads.

"Good evening, gentlemen," said May brightly, stopping in the middle of the room and spinning to look at each soldier in turn. "We have some visitors for you tonight. It's my cousin and her husband, as well as her friend. So please, do me a favor and show them how hospitable you all are." Her smile was contagious, and as she grinned at them each in turn, I saw her smile reflected, albeit far less energetically, in some of their faces.

Nathanial was already on his way over to speak to one certain gentlemen whose entire arm was bandaged, as well as part of his other hand.

"Don't worry too much about who it is," Irene said. "They'll all be happy to have someone to talk to, remember?"

With that, she made her way toward a younger man who was lying back in his bed, his arms tucked beneath his head, with a bandage over his eye.

I swallowed nervously, looking around.

There were two or three who were already asleep, even if the last light of day was still visible through the windows. Another had rolled away from us completely.

There was a young man nearest the fire who was sitting up in bed, reading a book. He had a bandage peeking out from underneath his striped pajamas.

He glanced up, likely feeling my gaze on him, and he smiled, his hazel eyes lucid and focused.

I wandered over to his bedside, standing at the foot of the metal frame. "Hello..." I said.

"Hello," he said in return. He had a nice voice, soothing and clear. And he was good looking, too. He couldn't have been older than twenty, maybe twenty-one.

My heart constricted when I saw the bandage beneath his shirt, as well as the scar across his upper lip that looked as if it had just begun to heal.

"My name is Helen," I said. "What's yours?"

"Jim," he said, smiling. "Jim Hopkins."

"Well, Jim," I said. "Do you mind if I sit with you for a bit? Keep you company?"

"Not at all," he said, closing his book and setting it down on the small, metal table beside his bed.

I sat down in the nearby folding chair, the metal cold beneath my skirt. "I'm sorry to have interrupted your reading," I said.

"Oh, that's all right," Jim said kindly, that smile never leaving his young face. "The nurses would have come in soon enough to check my bandages, so I wouldn't worry about it."

"May I ask what you were reading?" I asked, setting my purse down at the floor beside my feet.

"A book by Martin Luther," he said. "To be honest, I don't exactly have the patience for fiction these days. I would much rather read something that is edifying, and can help me grow even as I have to stay here recovering."

"That's admirable," I said. "Are you unhappy to be here recovering?" I asked.

He shook his head. "No, I didn't mean it like that. I just know that it will likely be some time before I'm able to return home, so I thought I might as well make the most of it."

"I think that's wonderful," I said.

"And what about you, Helen?" he asked. "Do you live here in Brookminster?"

"I do, yes," I said. "But I have only recently moved here."

"Ah, I see," he said. "Where did you come from?"

"I was born in Plymouth," I said. "Lived there most of my life."

"Plymouth?"

The voice was new, one I had never heard. The face of a man who couldn't have been much older than Jim leaned forward in the bed beside Jim's, curiosity written all over his pale face.

"I'm from Plymouth, as well," the young man said, laying a bandaged hand over his heart.

When he told me what street he had grown up on, my

own heart skipped. "That's very near where my parents live," I said. "We must have been neighbors."

"What an amazing coincidence," he said. "My name is Frank Mead."

"Mead?" I asked, astonished. "Is your father Daniel?"

The boy threw back his head and laughed. "Yes, he is!" he said.

"My name is Helen Lightholder," I said. "But my maiden name was Bennett."

"So then your father is James?" he asked.

It was my turn to laugh. "Yes, that's right!" I said.

He and I grinned at one another.

Jim looked back and forth between the two of us. "My, what a small world it is."

"I was just thinking the same thing," I said.

We spent the next quarter of an hour sharing stories from back home. It seemed I had been there more recently than he had, and I told him all about how things had been when I had moved.

"Old Mrs. Willard still sits out on her porch every morning, yelling at the children playing in the street," I said. "Especially those Woolfard boys. They can be quite a nuisance."

"And what about Sammy Lincoln? Last I heard, he'd come down with some terrible sickness. And with his father serving in the army..." Frank said, his voice trailing off.

"He was just fine when I left," I said, smiling. "Seems he took a turn for the better just before Christmas."

The relief was clear on Frank's face.

Then color appeared in his cheeks, and he ran a nervous hand over the back of his neck.

"And, um...what might you know about Emily Nichols?" he asked, not meeting my eye.

A sly grin appeared on Jim's face. "Is that the girl you're sweet on?" he asked.

"Shut it," Frank snapped, his face reddening further. He turned his eyes up hopefully to me. "Is she doing all right?"

I smiled at him, nodding my head. "She is in good health. My sister is very good friends with her sister, in fact. I know the Nichols family quite well."

Frank's eyes widened. "You do?"

"What's the matter with you?" Jim asked, falling back against his pillows and laughing. "I've never seen you like this before."

Frank looked sheepish. "I...well, my plan was to propose to her...but then I had to leave for the war..." he looked sadly down at his bandaged hand. "My hope is that I'll be able to return to Plymouth one day, so I can do what I planned to."

Jim grinned. "Now I know who you've been writing all those letters to in the dead of night when you think no one's awake," he said. "What's she like?"

Frank looked over at me, and a small grin appeared on his face. "Well...she's wonderful. I've never met anyone else like her in my life. She is smart, funny, and has a singing voice that angels would long for. She is stunning, as well, with hair so blonde it reminds me of the moonlight, and – "

A blood curdling scream echoed from somewhere

further inside the mansion, bouncing off the walls, and making the glass on the windows tremble.

Everyone fell silent.

My heart pounded, the blood rushing through my ears. Eyes fixed on the door, I realized I wasn't breathing, either.

The scream was followed by despairing sobs, which hung in the air, heavy and morose.

"...I think that was Lance," Jim said in a still, small voice, making me jump as he broke the silence.

"Lance?" I asked.

Frank nodded. He had swung his legs over the side of his bed so he could see Jim and me better. His gaze flickered out toward the hall. "His whole platoon was killed. He's the only one who survived."

Guilt crashed against my soul like a wave breaking on the rocky shore. How had I so easily forgotten where I was, and with whom I was speaking? These boys had just come from the front lines of war. They had seen terrible things, witnessed atrocities that no one should ever have to...

I let out a shaky breath, my heart rate beginning to slow. "I'm so sorry..." I said. "With all of this talk of home and familiar faces, I forgot that – "

"It's all right," Jim said, looking up at me with more wisdom in his face than men thrice his age. "We like to forget about it sometimes, too."

I gave him a sad, regretful sort of tight smile. "Is he... Lance, I mean...is he having nightmares?" I asked.

Jim sighed heavily, exchanging a glance with Frank. "Well...yes, and no," he said.

"Lance is living his nightmares, in a way," Frank said slowly. "There are several soldiers here who have essentially lost sense of themselves. When we go in to speak with them, it's almost as if they don't even hear you. They just lie there, staring at the ceiling, as if they are ignoring you..."

"And then, every once in a while, they have these outbursts, just like that," Jim said. "They believe they are back on the battlefield, and it doesn't matter if they are injured or not, they will fight."

"We've heard glass breaking, and metal slamming...I guess it can be quite brutal," Frank said.

"Would it help if someone came to speak with them?" I asked. "Someone like myself, or the friends that I arrived with?"

Frank shook his head, his eyes widening. "No, you wouldn't want to go in there, especially not now," he said.

"Those men have attacked the nurses," Jim said. "I even heard that Carlisle near put a knife in his own wife's chest...he couldn't recognize her. They believe they are still in the war. Their minds have gone. They believe that everyone else is the enemy, and they are just doing what they were trained to."

I swallowed hard, my heart aching. How terrible it was that these men gave up everything to protect our country...and this was the life they would have to suffer with in exchange.

It wasn't fair.

"But that's not the worst of it..." Jim said, his voice low. "One of the soldiers managed to escape."

"I wouldn't have wanted to meet him in the darkness," Frank said.

"That was the doctors' fear as well," Jim said. "What if he attacked someone? He would stop at nothing to kill if he believed the person might have been his enemy."

My stomach dropped.

"When, exactly, did this soldier escape from the hospital?" I asked.

7

Jim and Frank looked at one another. Frank's brow furrowed, and Jim's lips parted as he mouthed words, as if listing something in his mind.

"Well, I cannot be sure of the precise date," Frank said. "But it couldn't have been more than a week ago."

"I think it was even less than that," Jim said. "Five days at most, I believe."

My heart skipped.

It was far too much of a coincidence, wasn't it? These poor, delirious men...what if the one who had escaped had stumbled upon the Polish refugee, who had no place to go, and nowhere to hide? If so many other people in town had suspected he was German...how much more would a soldier without his wits believe it as well?

"You look troubled," Frank said. "What's wrong?"

"It's – " I said, wondering how much I should tell these boys. I decided it was best not to voice my theory just yet...not when I had so little information. It was far too easy to let the mind run away with its own fears. "What happened to the soldier?" I asked. "How and where did they find him?"

"Well, I was awake the night it happened," Jim said. "It must have been close to four in the morning when they noticed he was gone. The nurses were just finishing their shifts, and they always make the rounds to check on their patients before they retire for the evening. I heard whispers at first, but they became more frantic. Soon after, I heard a pair of them talking outside in the hall. They said one of the patients was missing from his bed. Well, that began quite the search. They were known to wander sometimes, but it was usually never far from their room. They searched the whole house, top to bottom, though, and were unable to locate him. It was then that they found the back door cracked open, someone having forgotten to lock it that day..."

"It took them the better part of the next day to find him," said Frank. "It seems he had wandered all the way down the road into the village. They found him passed out along the side of the road, covered in mud and goodness knows what else...it seems he injured himself somehow, as well, or reopened one of his gunshot wounds, because there was blood all over his hospital gown."

Blood. Just like the beggar, who was also covered in blood when they found him...

"The problem is that they will never know what happened to him," Jim said. "Or what he thinks might have happened. They've tried to ask him why he escaped like he did, but he can't seem to understand their questions."

"Did they inform the police about all this?" I asked.

Frank shrugged his shoulders. "All we know about what happened is what we have overheard the nurses and doctors saying. He's now been confined to a room, and spends most of his day sedated. They're hoping that once his wounds heal, and he isn't losing so much blood, that they'll be able to get someone in here to talk with him, maybe help open him up somewhat."

"I'm sorry you had to hear all that," Jim said with an apologetic smile. "The rest of us are pretty decent chaps, though. We won't mistake you for the enemy. I promise you that."

I smiled at him. "I know you won't."

Soon after, Nathanial and Irene were ready to leave, not wanting to stay away too long while a neighbor sat at the house with their son.

"Thank you, both, for such a pleasant time," I told Jim and Frank.

Frank beamed up at me. "Next time you write home, make sure you tell your sister to tell her friend to tell her sister that you met me."

I laughed. "I'd be happy to do so."

I shook hands with Jim, since Frank's was bandaged.

"Thank you for taking the time to spend the evening with us," he said, and his earnest tone gripped my heart. He squeezed my hand. "It was nice to discuss something completely ordinary for once. Perhaps I will dream of more mundane things tonight."

"I know I certainly will," Frank said with a laugh.

I promised them both I would return to visit as soon as I was able, and left with Irene and Nathanial.

We climbed into the car, my mind whirling.

"...Helen?" Irene asked.

"Yes?" I asked, my eyes snapping up to her in the front seat.

She gave me an apologetic look. "Are you all right? I've been asking you about those boys for the last few minutes. I suppose you haven't heard me?"

"Oh, I'm sorry," I said. "I was just thinking about some of the things I had talked about with them..."

"These soldiers...it just breaks my heart," Irene said as Nathanial pulled the car down the drive into the night. "They're so kind, though. I hope they get to go home once they've healed."

"One of the boys I was talking with was from my hometown," I said. "We knew the same families."

"Isn't that funny?" Nathanial said, glancing at me in the rearview mirror. "How small the world can seem at times."

"They also told me that one of the patients escaped a few nights ago..." I said, nervously licking my lips. "Remember the one we heard screaming?"

"Oh, yes," Irene said. "That was tragic, wasn't it? It broke my heart to hear that."

"You're saying one of them got out?" Nathanial asked. "How?"

"Well, according to the men I was speaking with, there are some soldiers at the hospital that have essentially lost their minds. They don't know who they are, or where they are. They live perpetually in their nightmares," I said.

"How terrible," Irene said. "No wonder that poor

fellow sounded so distraught..."

I nodded. "They also have been known to attack nurses, as well as their own family who come to see them."

"Really?" Nathanial asked. "Well, I suppose if they've taken leave of their senses, then I can see how they might think that those coming toward them are trying to attack them."

"And one of these men managed to escape from the hospital?" Irene asked. "Where is he now?"

"Oh, they found him," I said. "But he had been gone for a whole day. They discovered he was gone in the middle of the night almost five days ago...and then found him the next morning, covered in blood and mud, on the side of the street outside of town. He was unconscious."

"Do they have any idea what happened to him?" Nathanial asked.

"No," I said. "And they likely never will, because the soldier probably doesn't even remember, and cannot communicate it, either." I sighed. "The boys I was talking with said they would not have wanted to meet a soldier like him out in the street in the middle of the night. These men are trained to kill, and they seem to believe that many people are their enemies, unknowingly attacking those who are trying to help. And that got me thinking..."

"About what?" Irene asked.

"...that poor Polish beggar," I said in a quiet voice. "We all know that he was killed, but not how."

Irene turned around and looked at me, her eyes wide and face rather pale. "You cannot be serious," she said.

"The thought had never crossed my mind until those boys said the soldier had escaped just a few days ago... and it may have very well been the next day when the beggar's body was found in the Englewood's shed," I said. "It's far too much of a coincidence, if you ask me."

Irene looked over at her husband, whose face was now set in a hard, unflinching line.

"That is a troubling thought," Nathanial said.

"But wouldn't the hospital have worked with the police already?" Irene asked. "Surely they would have asked for their help in locating the soldier in the first place."

"I imagine they would have, yes," Nathanial said. "But even still..."

"What are you thinking?" I asked.

"I'm wondering if this might be something we should take to the police anyways," Nathanial said. "Because I would sleep much better at night knowing there isn't some mad, murderous fool roaming our streets at night."

Irene nodded, concern etched on her pretty, round face. "Very well, dear." She looked back at me. "Are you willing to tell the police what you heard?"

I nodded. "I do hope those boys will forgive me for sharing what they told me."

"If it is to help uncover a man's killer, I'm certain they will understand," she said.

I hoped she was right.

"Let me stop in and explain things to the neighbor we left sitting with Michael," Nathanial said. "Then we can go down to the station and inform Inspector Graves of our findings."

My heart clenched as I thought of Sam Graves, and of his gruff attitude toward me. He had specifically warned me to stay out of this whole situation. What was he going to do when I showed up at the police station with a theory of my own?

THE LOOK ON INSPECTOR GRAVES' face when we walked into his office was precisely what I expected it would be.

"Mrs. Lightholder," he said, his bright blue eyes narrowing. "What a surprise..."

Nathanial gave me a curious, sidelong look.

"What can I do for you three at such a late hour?" Sam asked, taking a seat in his leather chair behind his desk. He gestured for Irene and me to sit across from him.

"We went to the hospital tonight to visit with the wounded soldiers and deliver some supplies to the nurses," Nathanial said. "While we were there, Helen had an interesting conversation with some of the wounded."

"Did you, now?" Sam asked, his eyes narrowing even further. "Why do I get the feeling that I am not going to like the answer to my next question?"

I shifted uncomfortably in the chair. I could feel Irene's curious gaze upon me. I hadn't told her about my past interactions with Sam Graves, nor the clear warning he had given me in the cemetery the afternoon of the beggar's funeral.

"What did you hear?" he asked.

"I was told about a soldier that escaped," I said, and

shared with him the same story the boys had shared with me.

"And why, exactly, did you come all the way down here at nearly half past ten in the evening to tell me this?" he asked.

"Because I believe the soldier escaped the same night that the beggar was killed," I said. "And from what the boys told me, if they suspected he was an enemy for even a moment, he wouldn't have hesitated to attack."

I expected Sam to scold me and send me away.

Instead, though, he leaned back in his seat, regarding me with something between admiration and hostility. I wasn't sure which he was leaning toward for a few uncomfortable moments as he sat there, silent.

"You seem to have a mind for this sort of work, Mrs. Lightholder," Sam said with apparent reluctance. "Sniffing up clues wherever they might be found, putting the pieces together like a puzzle...never resting until the answer has been discovered, the truth on display for all to see."

I felt Irene's gaze on me, but I didn't look at her.

Sam pushed himself up out of his chair, his hands flat on the desk.

"You should know that we followed that lead already," he said, his eyes never leaving mine. "Three days ago, in fact. While half of my men were out looking for this escaped loon of a soldier, I was dealing with the body of some unfortunate beggar who had been bothering the townsfolk for almost a fortnight. Upon comparing stories, many of the officers came to the same conclusion you did, and we investigated."

He turned around to his window, his reflection looking irritated. He stared out into the darkness for a moment before his reflection shifted its gaze back to me.

"The soldier was not the one who killed the beggar," Sam said finally, clasping his hands behind his back.

"But they both were covered in blood – how can we be sure the soldier's blood wasn't just his own, but the beggar's as well?" I asked

"How do you know his body was bloody?" Sam asked, suddenly alert.

I shrunk a bit beneath his scrutiny, but I wasn't going to let him push me around.

I sat up straighter, glowering up at him.

"I saw the body in the shed," I said, meeting the gaze of his reflection.

He spun around, his real eyes fixed on me now.

"When did you do that?" Nathanial asked, astonished. "You were standing with me the whole time."

I looked sheepishly up at him. "I...sneaked around to the back and looked inside. I was worried it might have been someone I knew, and – "

"She can't resist prying into other people's business..." Sam interrupted. "It seems to be a trait that runs in the family..."

My cheeks burned, and I glared up at him.

"For your information, the blood the soldier had on his clothing was from his own wounds which had reopened in his effort to escape. The nurses believe that he must have thought he had been captured by the enemy, and was trying to get away. A gunshot, apparently.

A rather nasty one that was not healing well, due to his excessive outbursts."

I dipped my head at his words. Jim and Frank had said as much, that it might have been his own blood.

"Besides, he was found a long way from where we discovered the body of the beggar," Sam said. "Too far to make any logical sense that they had anything to do with one another. It was nothing more than a coincidence that both of those incidents happened on the same day."

"I see..." I said.

"I understand your desire to find an answer, but as I have told you, it should be left to the police. These investigations are dangerous, as you learned yourself the hard way with your encounter with Mrs. Martin. Your involvement would be nothing more than a liability. You really must keep your distance."

He shifted his gaze over to Irene.

"You two are friends?" he asked.

"Yes," Irene said, nodding.

"Then I would ask you to convince Mrs. Lightholder to keep well clear of all this. It will only end in her getting hurt."

Irene looked nervously over at me, and then up at her husband.

Nathanial cleared his throat, shifting his weight on his feet. "Not to be a bother, sir, but we are troubled by the idea of the killer not being found, as well," he said. "We have a young boy at home, and I for one am none too keen on the idea of someone else ending up dead."

Sam looked at Nathanial, his gaze hard, yet fair. "I understand," he said. "And we are doing our best to keep everyone in the village safe. That is our top priority. I can assure you both that we will make certain whoever did this does not go undiscovered. Now...if you will all excuse me, I have one more thing I must take care of this evening before I leave for the day."

He walked us back to the front door, and his goodbye was stilted and overly formal.

We weren't even two steps down the road before Irene turned to me, prodding me in the arm with her finger. "Helen, what were you thinking?" she asked in a very motherly tone. "Trying to get involved in a murder case? After everything you've been through?"

My cheeks burned, and I didn't know how to reply. I hadn't expected Sam Graves to treat me like a child and order Irene to turn on me like she was now.

"And going to look at that body like that?" Irene asked, shuddering. "Are you really sure that was wise?"

"I..." I started. "That poor beggar...he was looking for someone. His wife, his daughter, a friend...I don't know, but he was harmless. All he wanted was some help. And then someone comes along and just..." I couldn't get the words out. "And then leaves him in a shed so thought-lessly...it just sickens me, and I couldn't stand the thought of him being alone and without any help."

Irene's face fell, and she laid a hand on my arm. "I can understand that."

"That man probably had a family," Nathanial said. "People that would be devastated to know that this happened to him. And now they likely won't ever find out."

"Maybe it's better that way," Irene said. "Would you

rather spend your life not knowing, but still hopeful? Or would you rather know the truth?"

"The truth," I said. "Hope is a wonderful thing, don't get me wrong, but I would much rather know what happened so that I could grieve properly. As hard as it was, I'm glad I found out about Roger. I can't imagine the anguish I would have felt if I was waiting around for years and years for him to come home, and I just never knew."

"Yes, I suppose you're right," Irene said.

"And what if his family does come looking for him eventually?" I asked. "Wouldn't it be better to find justice for him?"

"I don't disagree with you," Irene said. "But wouldn't it be best to leave it to the police, allow them to solve the crime themselves?"

"Perhaps..." I said.

"Helen, please promise me that you won't put yourself in danger," Irene said. "You are far too dear a friend now for us to lose you. My heart nearly failed me when we learned about Mrs. Martin coming after you the way she did..."

As we came to a stop outside their front door, I hugged Irene.

"I promise I will stay out of harm's way," I said, smiling at her. "And thank you for tonight. I'm glad we had a chance to spend some time with those young men."

"Well, I'm glad you came along, as well," Irene said.

We wished each other good night, and I started up the road to my own house.

My mind was reviewing the evening, trying to digest everything I had seen and heard.

For a brief moment, I thought I had perhaps solved the poor beggar's murder. Yet I was back at square one again.

No, you're not back at square one, I said to myself sternly. *You are not getting involved. From here on out, you are not going to chase after this any further. Not only would it upset Irene, but it would make Sam Graves even more annoyed than he already is.*

I did my best not to think of those poor soldiers as I went to sleep that night, about the horrors they'd seen, and the nightmares they had to endure over and over again...

"War is a terrible thing..." I muttered to myself in the dark. "It will be better for everyone once it is finally over."

8

A rriving home so late the night before, I didn't manage to get a great deal of sleep. My alarm clock started to sing far too early, startling me out of a deep, dreamless sleep.

I rose for the day rather unhappily, dragging myself to the shower so that I could stand in the hot water, which did nothing to help me feel more awake. I washed my hair, dried it, and managed to tie it in a short braid before wrapping it into a knot at the nape of my neck.

I chose the most comfortable heels I owned, and decided to try a new dress that I had mended with some ribbons and new buttons. Wanting to model it for the customers I knew would come in that day, I hoped it might pique some of their interest so they might ask me about it.

My plan was to offer it to the customers as a possible future avenue for my shop. The idea of picking up Mrs. Martin's part of the market was growing on me, and I knew I would need to start somewhere. Why not with my own clothing?

I also knew that busying myself with the business that day would help distract me from thoughts about the beggar and his death. I wasn't sure why I couldn't shake it, but in a way, I almost felt responsible for what happened to him.

Now that it seemed the soldier who had broken out of the hospital probably had not been the one to kill the beggar, I found my thoughts drifting back toward the innkeeper. What if, in his anger, he had decided to take out his grief and rage over his son's death on a stranger?

I knew I could not entertain the idea of taking this possibility to Inspector Graves, especially not after bringing the theory about the soldier to him the night before. He would accuse me of further meddling and do everything he could to keep me out of the whole business.

Either way, I knew it wasn't my responsibility. Even if the possibility of the innkeeper being the killer seemed so plausible, I couldn't go and tell Sam that.

But why hasn't he gone to talk to him, yet? I wondered as I swept the floor of the shop a quarter of an hour before it opened. *This is a small village. It would surely be easy to find out how much Mr. Diggory despised the Germans. We weren't there more than half an hour before we learned about it...*

I had to force myself to stop thinking about it, as I knew it would distract me from all the other matters I had to tend to that day.

I opened the shop just after nine like I always did, and customers were arriving within just a few minutes.

"Oh, good, I was hoping you still had some gold zippers left at this length," said Mrs. Georgianna as she poured over the display that Sidney had repaired for me. "I'll have four, please."

"I'm afraid that I need another button mended," said poor Mr. Oliver, who was very nearly blind. "No one seems to do as good a job as you do."

"That's all right, dear, six brown buttons and six navy will be just fine. Not to worry," said Mrs. Trent.

It wasn't until almost noon when Sidney appeared at the back door of the shop that I realized why there were so many more customers than usual.

"Oh, well, surely you knew about the town festival?" he said as he carried his ladder in through the door; he had seen a leak in the ceiling the last time he was here, and seemed determined to fix it. "It happens every year in the third week of June."

"I've heard nothing of it," I said.

He grinned. "How did I, a man who has lived here for even less time than you have, manage to hear about this first?"

I smirked at him, folding my arms. "Very amusing. You know very well that I was only here a few weeks before you were."

He winked as he unfolded his ladder beneath the part of the ceiling that he wanted to inspect. "Regardless, it's supposedly a very important part of this town's history. According to a farmer I was working with earlier today, the festival began all the way back in the seventeenth century, as a way to celebrate a victory in battle. I can't remember which one, but it was a rather large event. It seems that the man who had supposedly inspired Robin Hood was in attendance during the archery competition."

"Good heavens, was he really?" I asked.

"Well, that one can never know for certain, but we can be sure that it is a long-lived tradition here in Brookminster, and everyone looks forward to it each year," he said.

I looked around the shop, seeing women bending their heads together, talking excitedly about their selection of ribbons, and another man attempting to find a silk tie that he liked.

"You think they are all preparing for the festival?" I asked.

"I thought you were doing the same," he said, glancing down at my dress. "That's quite a nice dress you've made for yourself."

I blushed as he turned, climbing up the ladder. "Thank you very much," I said, touching the scalloped collar that I had lined with silk ribbons. "I thought I might try something different."

"That farm you mentioned…" I said, keeping my eyes on the customers near the front of the store, in case any of them needed me. "Was that the farm you were at earlier this week?"

"Indeed," he said, shining his flashlight up into the beams of wood that ran the length of the ceiling, squinting. "The farmer asked if I might be able to help him repair his tractor."

"You can repair tractors, too?" I asked. "Is there nothing you can't do?"

He spared me a momentary grin. "Well, aren't you

kind? And yes, I actually started discovering I was rather handy when my uncle's tractor broke down when I was a lad. I was fascinated as he worked on it, and before I knew it, he let me help him and my cousins get it back up and running. From there, I moved onto cars, trucks, other farm equipment..."

He pressed his fingers up against the boards above his head, his brow furrowing.

"I'm not pleased with this," he said, shaking his head. "I'm afraid these might need to be replaced."

I sighed, shaking my head. "It's always something in this house, isn't it?"

"Well, you're certainly keeping me busy," he said, climbing back down the ladder.

"Yet you will not let me pay you," I said, arching an eyebrow.

He smiled, dimples appearing in his freckled cheeks. "You wait until I bring over every shirt I own and ask you to fix the buttons and the loose stitching on them all. It will be enough work for you for an entire week."

I laughed. "I suppose I shouldn't complain then, should I?"

"You are always welcome to, though I think that seems rather out of character for you," he said.

I smiled. There was something about Sidney Mason that I found very pleasant. I liked the way he so easily made me laugh.

Even though there was still a great deal about him that I was unfamiliar with, I realized that if he ever wanted to talk about his past, then he would when he was ready to.

"It must be terrible for a farmer to not have his tractor working," I said as I picked up an order form from the small stack I had accumulated on the back counter beside the till.

Sidney bent over his toolbox that he had stashed beneath the ladder, and lifted a pencil out, tucking it behind his ear. "It certainly is making life a bit difficult for him and his family," he said. "It's nearing harvest time, and he will be needing it then without a doubt. And with the rations and everyone's income meager, he can't afford to come into town to order the new parts he would need." He slid a hammer into his toolbelt, along with a couple of nails, which he dropped into the small pocket on his hip. "If I'm honest, though, what he needs is an entirely new tractor. I know he knows that as well, but it's simply out of the question for them right now."

"I can imagine..." I said.

"There is a great deal more pressure on farmers to produce enough crops this year," Sidney said, climbing back up the ladder to the ceiling. "Not only are they supplying food for the locals, but they're also under obligation to give a sizable portion to the military."

"I suppose that's not much of a surprise," I said.

"Even still, they aren't being paid nearly what they used to be for their goods, and to top it off, it seems they've been dealing with some thieves around their farm," Sidney said.

"Thieves?" I asked. "How terrible."

He nodded. "Yes, I thought so too...especially when I learned that one of them ended up being that Polish beggar."

It was as if I had swallowed a chunk of ice whole. "You're kidding..."

He shook his head. "I wish I was. The farmer asked if I'd seen the beggar in town, and I told him that he'd been killed. He seemed surprised, but also not very sympathetic. That's when he told me that the beggar had sneaked onto his properly in the middle of the night, and the farmer had caught him stealing from his family's personal store of food."

While I had not known the beggar at all apart from our meeting, the news was still somewhat of a shock to me. It took me a moment to realize that just because the man had been killed didn't necessarily mean that he had been a *good* man in the first place...as much as I had been believing he was the whole way through.

"I thought the police were supposed to help the poor beggar?" I asked.

"I thought so as well," he said. "I dropped him off there, but you heard how bad his English was. I'm assuming they were either unable to discern who it was he was looking for, or were simply unable to assist him. I would imagine they did their best to help him find a place to stay, maybe someplace where he could get food..."

I frowned. "Yes, and I think they stepped into a minefield unknowingly." I looked up at him, my heart sinking. "The innkeeper lost his son recently in the war, and is none too pleased to encounter anyone who is of German descent."

"So I've heard," Sidney said. "He's not the first I've met who feels that way. I can't say I wouldn't have been wary or concerned if that beggar had, in fact, been German instead of Polish."

I rubbed my arms nervously. "Nor I, I suppose."

"I can't be sure what happened next, though. My guess is that when the innkeeper chased him away, he needed to find something to eat. Unsurprisingly, there were many in town who wouldn't have wanted to help a German refugee, either. How could they have been certain he wasn't a spy or something akin to one?"

"But why had he wandered all the way out there to the farm?" I asked. "Was there no one in town willing to help him?"

"That was the farmer's same question," Sidney said, taking the pencil from his ear and marking the ceiling where he intended to cut it. "I guess the beggar tried to flee when the farmer caught him in the act, and the farmer took a shot at him with his hunting rifle as he fled."

I gasped. "He...what?"

"The beggar was trespassing," Sidney said, pulling a tape measurer from his toolbelt, unrolling it, and pressing it against the ceiling. He leaned back and stared at the length, likely discerning its measurement. "What would you do if you found someone had broken into your home in the middle of the night? Politely ask them to leave?" He sighed. "These are dark times we live in, and everyone is on edge. In many ways, we have no choice but to be wary of those we don't know, and our trust has to become more of a rarity."

"That's a rather sad way to view the world..." I said.

"Not everyone desires this war. And there are many parts of the world that are untouched by it, as well."

Sidney looked at me, and I was surprised to see a haunted expression in his eyes. "This war has touched us all, each and every person living today. I don't believe there is a soul alive who doesn't know someone lost in the war, or who hasn't had a loved one that was hurt or drafted or forced from their homes..." he said in a low voice. "I understand that my view may be a bit bleak, but I fear the world may never be the same after all this is over."

"It will come to an end, though," I said. "It has to."

"That is true," Sidney said, climbing down off the ladder. "I'm sorry if I upset you. It wasn't my intention."

"No, no, it's quite all right," I said. "It's just unfortunate that situations like the one that happened with the beggar have to occur even during times of war."

"Some might argue that these atrocities occur more often during times of difficulty," Sidney said. "We each feel a need to protect those we love, which is exactly why the farmer reacted the way he did."

"I suppose I cannot blame him for that," I said. "And to be honest, it makes me wonder if the beggar was as kind as I kept thinking he might be..."

"We may never know, honestly," Sidney said, grabbing a small notepad from his toolbox and scrawling down a few notes on it with measurements he'd taken. "What I do know is that there are people everywhere who need help, and there are still yet those who would like nothing more than to help, but their hands are tied behind their backs."

"I wish I knew more about this farmer's interaction with the beggar," I said. "Perhaps it would help point us in the direction of who his killer was? Or where he might have been heading afterward?"

"Well, you are welcome to come with me when I go back there this afternoon," he said. "I needed to retrieve some tools from home before returning to work on the tractor."

"Won't that seem strange, though? Just coming with you to speak with the farmer about the beggar?" I asked.

Sidney shrugged. "I suppose you won't have to be so forthright about why you are there. You've helped me on plenty of projects around your own house. I could simply say I thought it wise to bring in another set of hands to work."

I pursed my lips. "Sam Graves will certainly not be happy with me. Neither will Irene."

Sidney's brow furrowed. "Why not?"

"I promised them I would stop digging around about the beggar," I said. "But something tells me I'm rather close to uncovering the truth behind this bizarre mystery. And I intend to see it through to the end...for the dead man's sake."

9

I was still a little surprised that Sidney agreed to let me go with him. I thought for certain that as soon as I'd told him about Sam Graves telling me off for investigating in the first place, he would have urged me to keep my distance. And in many ways, I had almost hoped he would. It would have given me an excuse to stay out of it, and would have perhaps helped me to realize that it wasn't worth pursuing any further.

But Sidney's attachment to the beggar seemed to be very similar to my own. In a way, I wondered if we were the only ones who had tried to show kindness to the man.

I voiced that thought to Sidney as we drove over in his car later that afternoon, the sun hanging high in the sky above us. "We were the only ones who knew he was Polish, weren't we?"

His eyes were fixed on the road ahead of him, but I could see the tightness in his jaw, and the stiffness of his shoulder. "It's hard to believe, but perhaps we were. As I said earlier, everyone is wary of those they don't know. And with the war, and our enemies..."

"I know," I said.

"It's not fair. None of it is. But I suppose what's done is done, and while I agree that the poor man deserves justice, we may just have to realize that we might never find the answers we are looking for," Sidney said.

That was a troubling thought, but he was completely right. No matter how far we followed the trail, there might never be a resolution.

"Why are you so intent on finding an answer?" Sidney asked. "You hardly knew the man, right? What is so important about solving this mystery?"

"To be honest...I'm not exactly sure," I said. "I suppose that this war has taken people from me, and the idea of someone not knowing what happened to their father, or brother, or husband troubles me far too much. I want something to be set right in a world where everything, and every moment, could be turned upside down."

"I understand," Sidney said. "In a way."

He turned the car into a narrow, dirt drive that led away from the main road running out of town. We had to have been several kilometers away, as Brookminster had disappeared behind a low lying hill some time ago. We had been enjoying views of sheep grazing in lush, grassy fields, and rows of wheat that was still sprouting from the ground, several weeks from growing into its golden hue.

The car bumped along the uneven road, parts of which were filled with holes and patches of thick roots. I gripped the seat as Sidney did his best to navigate around the more difficult spots, and wondered just how far away from the road the farmhouse was.

It appeared over another hill, nestled between a handsome barn and a pair of silos. It was by no means the largest farm I had ever seen, but from what Sidney had described, I had imagined a poor, unfortunate little place.

The lonely, broken tractor was sitting among some untrimmed grass along the side of the house, the green metal that normally surrounded the engine lying on the ground, exposing all of the mechanical bits beneath it. Some rusted tools lay around it, and there was a small ladder leaning up against the body.

Sidney pulled the car up beside a rickety looking truck, painted a quaint pale blue. The wheel hubs were rusted, though, and the farm's name, *Maple Wood Grove,* had faded from the doors somewhat.

"Don't be too concerned if Mr. Cooke seems a bit gruff," Sidney said in a low voice as we made our way toward the front porch of the little cottage with ivy snaking up its stone walls, nearly obscuring the front bay window. "His wife is very sweet, and he's just difficult to read."

I nodded as he raised his hand and knocked on the door.

It was only a moment before the knock was answered by a kindly faced elderly woman with silvery hair pulled back in a loose bun behind her head. She wore a simple floral patterned dress and a pristine white apron. She smiled, her blue eyes bright as she recognized Sidney.

"Oh, Mr. Mason," she said. "I'm pleased you were able to come back so swiftly."

"Of course," he said, tipping his trilby hat to her and grinning his charming grin. "I only had to take care of a few minor things back at home, including helping with Mrs. Lightholder's ceiling which seems to be leaking." He gestured to me. "And she has offered to come help me with those last few things I needed to finish on the tractor today. I hope that's all right."

"That's perfectly fine," Mrs. Cooke said, smiling at me. "I think it's always good for a young woman to be able to get her hands dirty once in a while."

"I agree," I said. "Especially in these times."

"Indeed," she said. "Well, I'll just go get Freddie. He's been determined to stay in his study for the last week... it's rather surprising, really, because he has never been one to remain indoors when there is work to be done..." She shook her head. "My apologies. I won't bore you with our family troubles. Go on out back, he will meet you out there."

Sidney gave me a sidelong look as she closed the door behind us.

"She seems nice," I said.

"Yes..." he agreed. "Perhaps a bit more concerned than she was earlier."

"What do you mean?" I asked as we made our way around the outside of the house.

"Her husband was in his study when I arrived this morning as well," he said. "Said he was reading the papers. Mrs. Cooke told me that he spent a great deal of time brooding over the war. He can't seem to talk about anything else..."

"I thought she looked a bit worried for a moment," I said as we rounded the corner, the tractor coming back into view.

Sidney began to tell me what precisely needed to be fixed on the tractor, asking if I would be willing to unscrew the face plate of a piece of metal beside the seat, when footsteps sounded on the grass behind us.

"Sorry for keeping you waiting," said a rough voice. "Wasn't expecting you back here so soon."

"I suppose I should have let you know before I left that I intended to come back," Sidney said.

Mr. Cooke was a thin man, who looked as if he had missed one too many meals. His clothing hung off him, and the dark circles beneath his eyes told more about his exhaustion than his tired voice had.

His eyes drifted over to me, and his gaze hardened. "And who might you be?"

"I'm Helen Lightholder," I said, suddenly self-conscious about my presence here in the first place. "I thought I could come out here and help Sidney finish your tractor."

Mr. Cooke shifted his gaze toward Sidney. "I don't remember asking you to share our troubles with others," he said.

Sidney's face fell. "Oh...I am sorry, sir. I just thought having more hands might make the work go faster, allow you to get back to using your tractor sooner."

Mr. Cooke grunted, folding his arms. "I have plenty of

time still. And besides...it's given me time to catch up on all the happenings in the world."

Sidney gave me a knowing look before glancing back at Mr. Cooke. "That's good, I suppose. Would you possibly have a different sized wrench? I forgot mine back at home."

Mr. Cooke nodded. He disappeared a moment later, before returning with a few different sizes, all of which seemed rusted, as if they hadn't been used in years.

"Have you heard about what's happening overseas now?" Mr. Cooke asked, leaning up against the tractor as Sidney dislodged a piece of the engine. "It's terrible. The Germans are doing a real number on the Russians."

"So I hear," Sidney said with some strain, his fingers pulling the next piece of the engine off. The piece was shattered, with a sizable hole in the side. "I believe this is your problem, Mr. Cooke. But luckily for you, I think with some basic welding, it should be easy enough to fix."

"Glad to hear it," he said. "It's always good when things work out in our favor, isn't it? When things are put back in order, or go as they should?"

"Of course," Sidney said. "That's the ideal outcome in every situation, isn't it?"

"Precisely," he said. "That's why I believe we'll be the ones to win this war in the end."

"I for one am hoping for a swift end to the war," Sidney said. "I'm looking forward to life returning to some semblance of normalcy. As I'm sure you are, as well."

"Of course," he said. "And I'll be rejoicing when our enemies have to answer for their crimes." His face darkened as he stared at some distant spot on the ground. "Did I tell you that one of those blasted German refugees sneaked onto my property, and was stealing from me?"

My heart skipped as I stared at him. His eyes were wide, and had taken on a wild appearance. The knuckles on his fingers were the color of bone.

Sidney sat back on his heels, glancing up at Mr. Cooke. He opened his mouth to answer, but Mr. Cooke continued on.

"And he wasn't just stealing food. Oh, no. When I found him, he was in the garage, going through my tools. He'd filled a sack with there's no telling what, but he was also holding a scythe that I was in the process of mending," he said. "It was the dead of night, and all it would have taken was him to have any sort of knowledge of locksmithing, and he would have easily been able to get into the house."

I sat stock still beside the tractor seat, two of the screws of the plate Sidney had asked me to unscrew resting on my palm, the screwdriver poised over the third. I didn't even need to ask about the beggar. Mr. Cooke was so upset about it still that he willingly brought it up, even knowing that the man was dead.

"I heard noises from the garage. I grabbed my rifle, thinking it might be a raccoon or some other creature that was looking for food..." Mr. Cooke said, a growl in his voice. "Imagine my surprise when I found a ragged man on the other side of the door, likely with the intention of breaking down my door and coming in to harm my family?"

"Mr. Cooke, if I may be so bold..." Sidney said, getting

to his feet. I noticed his fingers were covered in engine grease when he pulled a handkerchief from his pocket and began to clean his hands. "We don't know that the beggar you met was a dangerous person. What's more, he wasn't even German. He was Polish."

Mr. Cooke's body went rigid.

"I realized after our conversation this morning that I should have told you that earlier," Sidney said. "I understand it is easy to make that mistake, as many in town have as well. But he was no German."

"Well..." Mr. Cooke said, his voice even more of a growl. "Regardless, he still broke into my garage, and was stealing from me."

"Do not mistake me, sir," Sidney said. "I believe wholeheartedly that what he did was entirely wrong. No matter what his lot in life, there was no rhyme or reason for him to do what he did."

"That's right," Mr. Cooke said with a nod. "That's precisely what I thought."

He shifted his weight, his gaze narrowing as he looked down at Sidney.

"How did you know he wasn't German?" he asked.

Sidney met his gaze with ease. "I have friends in Poland. I recognized some of the words he used."

"I see..." Mr. Cooke said.

He glanced down at the tractor, and the broken part in Sidney's hand.

"The sun's going to set soon," Mr. Cooke said. "I think it would be best if the two of you were on your way."

Sidney glanced at me for a brief moment. "It won't

take me long to get this fixed up, sir, if you just wanted me to – "

"I don't," Mr. Cooke said. "Now that I see the problem, I can fix it myself."

The tension between us was tangible, so thick that it was like a dark cloud that had settled over us, swollen with rain and thunder, just waiting to unleash itself upon us.

"Very well," Sidney said, laying the part that needed to be fixed upon the seat of the tractor, and picking up his tools from the ground. He looked at me and nodded toward the car. "If you need anything else, Mr. Cooke. You know where I am."

Mr. Cooke let out a noncommittal grunt, not bothering to lift his eyes from the ground.

We headed back down the dirt lane toward the main road a few minutes later, bumping along through the holes and ditches of the drive.

"That was quite a surprise," I said in a small voice.

"Indeed it was," Sidney said. His face was hard, and his gaze distant. "Something was strange."

"It was almost as if he felt guilty for believing the beggar to be something he was not," I said.

"I thought the same," Sidney said.

"I just can't believe that even though the beggar is gone, there is still such a great deal of turmoil surrounding his appearance in the village. Why? Why was it such a troubling occurrence for so many who live in Brookminster?" I asked.

Even as the words left my mouth, I knew the answer.

"...Because of the war," I said before Sidney could. "Because of the unrest."

"I know," he said. "It's all very unsettling. I'm sorry it's troubling you so much."

I sat in silence until we returned to the edge of town.

"Helen..." Sidney said. "I think that I have to agree with Irene, and Sam Graves... I think it would be wise if you were to leave any more investigating about the beggar to the police."

I wasn't entirely surprised to hear him say that. It was something I had begun thinking since hearing Mr. Cooke's story about finding the beggar in the garage.

"I'm just worried that you might end up getting hurt. Whoever it was that took the life of that beggar... I'm afraid that if you continue to go down this road, you might – "

"Get hurt," I said, looking up at him, trying to force a smile. "I know. Just like last time."

He gave me a knowing, tight half-smile.

"Yes," he said. "Just like last time."

10

I knew that I had agreed to keep my distance. I knew that Sidney, and Irene, and Sam Graves had all warned me to stay away from these dangerous situations. After hearing the farmer's angry reaction about the beggar, I wanted nothing more than to distance myself from it as well.

And yet...I found I could think of little else.

Perhaps my determination to have all of my questions answered was a fault, a rather debilitating weakness in my life. I could certainly see how others might think that. I, however, knew that it was something about me that I had wrestled with all my life, and ultimately, the answers I sought were for good reason. I knew they would absolutely drive me mad if left unresolved.

And that was why I found myself at the scene of the crime once again, in the dead of night, with nothing but a flashlight clasped tightly in my hand to keep me company.

I was quite literally losing my mind, I was well aware

of it. What was it about this poor beggar that was keeping me from sleeping? Why was I so focused on his death, just like I had been with my aunt's? And Roger's?

Thinking of Roger made my face flush as I crept around the corner of the butcher's house. Would there ever be a time in my life where I didn't think of him like that?

The shed where the beggar's body had been found stood where it always did, shrouded in shadow, without a soul in sight. The caution tape had been removed, and if someone was unaware of the tragedy that had occurred, it would have been nothing more than a simple, rather rickety garden shed.

The dewy grass muffled the sounds of my footsteps as I tiptoed across the lawn, keeping my ears perked in case anyone else was out this late. The air was cool, and the wind bit through the knit sweater I wore.

My breath caught in my throat as a rustle in the grass behind me made me freeze. My heart hammered as I glanced over my shoulder.

No one was standing there, and as I looked up and down the path, I didn't see any other people, either.

I swallowed hard, and nearly ended up swallowing my tongue as another rustle made me blanch.

A tuft of grass along the path behind the houses trembled, and a moment later, an orange tabby cat launched itself from inside, taking off into the night.

I sagged against the wall of the shed, my hand clutching my heart that threatened to beat right out of my chest. *It was just a cat...* I thought.

I scolded myself, telling myself to turn around and make my way back home. But the small, curious voice in the back of my mind responded with a simple statement; *But I'm already so close. What could looking in for just a moment hurt?*

I walked around to the front of the shed, shining the flashlight up at the handle. There was no lock, and when I rested my hand on the cold, metal knob, I realized it would give easily.

I half expected the inside to smell rancid, and the blood to still be coating the floorboards...but it wasn't. There was nothing more than a musty, unused smell hanging in the air, and the floor had been scrubbed clean somehow. There was no evidence that a dead body had been there just a number of days ago.

I shone the narrow beam of light around the shed, looking for anything that seemed out of place. I wondered what had happened to all the items that the beggar had stolen, the goods that he had taken from the farmer. I was curious about what he would have wanted for himself, though it was likely all now at the police station, kept away as evidence, never to be seen again.

I used the tip of my shoe to move aside an old, worn tarp, yet found nothing more than some rusted garden tools and a pair of buckets. The shelves along the back wall were relatively bare as well, holding nothing more than a few terracotta pots, faded from years of use, and a pair of thick, leather gloves.

I sighed. There was nothing here. No further clues. Nothing to indicate that the beggar had ever been here.

Yet, even as I stood there, a chill ran down my spine. A

cold, uncomfortable prickle rose up on the back of my neck.

Even if there was no evidence of a death, it did not change the fact that a body had been lying in here, transforming it from nothing more than an innocent place for garden tools, to a final resting place for a human being.

It was a bone chilling thought.

Had he been killed here in the shed? Was he killed somewhere else and then dragged away, deposited here to throw the police off the trail?

My head throbbed as I worked through all these new questions. It was almost as if every time I thought I was taking a step forward, I was in fact taking four steps backward.

*I should just give up...*I thought. *This is likely a sign that I am delving into something too deep that really does not concern me...*

I frowned. But this did concern me...at least to an extent.

I couldn't be completely sure why, but I realized in that moment, standing in that dark, dreary shed, that I felt guilty about his death...responsible even.

That was why I was pursuing this case as much as I was. That was why I had gone to the funeral, and sought answers from the farmer.

I felt responsible for the Polish man's death...because I had been unable to help him in life.

What could I have done differently? I asked myself as I stepped back out into the night, slowly pulling the door of the shed behind me. It wasn't as if I knew Polish, or would have been able to speak it. He was a vagabond, wandering around, seemingly harassing many of the people in Brookminster.

But what if Sidney and I had been able to help him that day? Should I have taken him in, and helped him search for whatever it was that he was looking for? Would Sidney have been able to help and protect the man from the scrutiny of the local people?

Maybe he wouldn't have been starving. Maybe he wouldn't have seen the need to break into the farmer's garage. Maybe he wouldn't have harassed the innkeeper, provoking him to anger?

These were all questions I'd never get the answer to. All I had was regret in knowing that maybe, just maybe, I could have done more, and simply did not.

As I made my way back toward home, I found my thoughts drifting toward how terrible the world was in general as of late. Was it always this way, and I had simply remained ignorant of it?

It must have been, at least in a way. There were always terrible people, and always difficulties. War seemed to exacerbate these issues, making them far more prominent than they normally were. Drastic life changes, like death and birth, were a great deal more frequent during the war. We heard about little else but the sheer numbers of those who had lost their lives.

I thought of Roger, and all he sacrificed. I thought of the young men at the hospital, and how their lives would never be the same after entering the war.

These dreary thoughts followed me home. They clung to my mind all night long. They lingered the next morning when I went to visit Irene, knowing that I needed help getting out of my own mind.

"I think you need to make the choice to put all this behind you," Irene said as she set down a steaming cup of tea in front of me, concern written all over her pretty, round face. "I care for you, which is why I feel the need to tell you that you have invested far too much of yourself into these matters, and I'm worried for you."

I silently picked up the sugar and lowered a few cubes into my cup, swirling the amber liquid around with my spoon. She was right...I just did not want to admit it.

Irene sighed heavily, taking a seat across from me. "I can understand why you feel the way you do. Whenever we go through something difficult, there are always ways that we wish we could improve our actions. With the beggar, though, there is nothing you could have done differently, dear."

"But what if I had?" I asked. "What if I had done more to help?"

"What if he was not as kind and as wholesome as you are determined to believe he was?" Irene asked, becoming cross. "What if he was a wicked man who wanted nothing more than money that he could use to spend on drink?"

I licked my lips, unable to answer.

"Think about it," she said. "He was harassing the innkeeper. He stole from the farmer. He wandered around this town, supposedly looking for someone...and what proof do we have aside from what Sidney has told us?"

"Why would the beggar lie to us, though?" I asked.

"Because he was hungry?" Irene asked, shrugging her shoulders. "I don't like to think about people in such stark terms either, but his actions speak loudly for him."

"You didn't see the look on his face when I met him," I said in a low voice. "He meant what he said. He really was looking for someone – "

"But you don't know who that is," Irene said. She sighed, wiping down the table with the cloth in her hand out of habit, absentminded. "I'm sorry, Helen...I just don't think that you need to worry yourself silly over this man like you are. With your aunt, I could completely understand that you were concerned, especially given the fact that you are living in her home. But with this beggar...you have no connection to him, aside from your own compassion and heartache. What happened was tragic, of course. But I think that it would really be best if you put this behind you, make peace with it, and move on."

I swallowed hard, hearing the words and agreeing with them deep in my heart, even if they stung. "I know," I said. "I think you're right."

She laid a hand on my shoulder, squeezing it affectionately. "I don't mean to upset you. I hope you know that."

"I do," I said. "And thank you."

I watched her walk toward the front door, getting ready to open the tea house for the day. There were already some customers milling around outside, waiting for their hot, morning tea.

It suddenly felt as if everyone else was against me. I knew that Irene meant well, and that she knew me well enough now to know my heart was in the right place.

But she was right.

This was where I would step down.

I had no choice. There was nothing else to go on. This mystery, just like the mystery surrounding Roger's death, would likely never be resolved.

That was aggravating...but it was the truth.

And I could do nothing but accept it.

11

A s reluctant as I was to put the whole situation behind me, I found a weight had been lifted from my shoulders, nonetheless. Perhaps the feeling that I had been partially responsible for the beggar's death had been what was keeping me tied to the case, and after Irene helped me to see that it wasn't my fault, I was able to look at the whole thing a bit more clearly.

I realized that one of the ways that I would hopefully be able to get past the whole thing was if I were to go and pay my final respects to the beggar. If I could form my own fears into words, even knowing that he would never hear them, or ever have been able to understand them, then maybe I'd be able to finally disconnect myself from him.

The air was sticky as I closed my shop the following afternoon. The clouds overhead were low in the sky, dark and moving rapidly toward the horizon. It would surely rain within the next hour or so.

I grabbed my umbrella and started down through the town.

The streets were almost entirely empty, likely due to the impending rain. I hadn't heard the dull rumble of a vehicle since that morning, and many windows were already aglow from the lights being turned on indoors.

The rains were beginning to patter down softly on the ground just as I ascended the rolling hill toward the church. I opened the umbrella just as I stepped through the open gates into the cemetery.

I always found churchyards so utterly quiet. Everything seemed so unnaturally still. It was as if the dead were simply waiting to be awakened again, as if the presence of the living would somehow stir them to life once more.

I wrapped my arm around myself, trying not to let the shivers overtake me.

The beggar's grave, I knew, was in the farthest corner, away from any other plots. He was buried all alone, never to be laid beside his family like he should have been.

As I made my way around the large tree that Sam Graves had been leaning against the last time I'd been here, I saw another person standing near the grave.

I ducked behind the tree, carefully peering around it.

It was Mr. Diggory, the innkeeper.

He didn't seem all that troubled by the rain that was beginning to fall more rapidly. He stood as still as the headstone he was staring at beneath his own umbrella, the rain rolling off and onto the ground below.

At first, I wondered if he was possibly visiting someone from his family. From this distance, I couldn't tell for certain, but the somber expression on his face made my initial fear pass away.

I stepped out from around the tree, and started toward him.

I wasn't all that far away from him when I realized that he was indeed standing in front of the beggar's grave.

He looked up at me briefly, and seemed only somewhat surprised to see me there.

"Good afternoon," he said in a low voice. All of the sourness that he'd expressed the last time I'd seen him was gone, replaced by a dejected tone.

"Hello," I said, standing nearby, but still giving him some space.

"It was Helen, correct?" he asked.

"Yes," I said.

He nodded. "I don't think we've properly met since you moved into the village. I'm Jonathon Diggory."

He held out his hand, which I took and shook.

"Helen Lightholder," I said. "It's a pleasure."

Mr. Diggory sighed rather heavily, shaking his head. "I can't say it's been much of a pleasure for anyone to be around me as of late..." he said, turning his gaze back to the headstone. "Not for my wife, or my oldest son...my usual customers haven't been coming around much lately, either."

"I'm sorry to hear that," I said.

He was silent for a few moments.

"I won't bother you..." I said softly. "I was just coming to pay my respects."

"That's precisely what I came to do as well," he said.

"It's something I have been meaning to do. I've been hoping it would help me to move past my son's death."

I looked over at him. I was certain he knew that most people in town were aware of his son's death. It would have been in the papers by now, and news like that traveled quickly in such a small village.

There was a hardness in his gaze as he stared down at the stone. He wrestled with something deep down within himself. His jaw was set, his stare fierce.

"It was the Germans," he said, a little more of an edge to his words. "I've been so angry at them since the start of the war, for taking my son away from us, but after his death, I – " His words caught in his throat.

My heart began to race. Was Mr. Diggory about to confess to a crime? Had I wandered into the cemetery at an inopportune time?

For the first time, I noticed the flowers in his hands. Wildflowers, perhaps even some picked from his own wife's garden. They were laden with water, drooping, with some of the petals lying down at his feet.

"Then this beggar appeared in town..." Mr. Diggory said with a short glance in my direction. "And he showed up at the back door of my inn, no less. To say I was troubled would be an understatement..."

I clutched the umbrella in my hands, wondering if it might be wise for me to just turn around and walk away, leaving him to deal with his mistakes on his own...if that was what he was trying to admit to me, as if I were some sort of priest.

"As soon as he opened his mouth, I thought he was a German spy. Disguising himself as a poor beggar, he would likely be able to soften the hearts of many. But our enemies are clever, and will use any means to undermine our soldiers, even something as dastardly as portraying themselves as the poor and infirm..." Mr. Diggory said.

Then his expression changed, which surprised me. The hard edge softened, and his brow fell, making him appear like no more than a frightened child.

"He came day after day, looking for something, or someone. I couldn't be sure. The first day, I refused him. The next, I found him going through the garbage behind the inn, so I gave him some stale bread and cheese that I'd picked the mold off of..." he said, staring down at his feet.

The rain began to fall harder, beating against our umbrellas as if they were drums.

"I quickly realized that he understood I would give him food if he continued to come around, but it wasn't as if I had a great deal of it to share. Between the rationing and the dip in visitors to the village who would stay at the inn, money has been a great deal tighter, and as charitable as I would typically be, I knew I couldn't afford it," he said. "But even still...in my heart, I knew that I didn't want to give to this man, this man who was possibly the enemy."

But he wasn't... I wanted to say. *At least...I don't believe he was the enemy you think he was.* I thought back to what Irene had said. How could I be certain that he wasn't hostile? Wasn't dangerous?

I wasn't. And even though that didn't make him *the* enemy, it certainly could have made him *an* enemy.

Mr. Diggory sniffed, rubbing his nose. "...Come to

find out the man was from Poland, so he couldn't have been a German spy. All that time, I'd been so wrongly accusing him of working alongside those – " He caught himself again, his face screwing up with effort. "I was having nightmares, thinking that this man knocking on my door every afternoon was the same man who shot my son's plane down out of the sky. As irrational as that was, I could think of little else. My business has suffered, as has my marriage…"

I wanted to reach out and lay a hand on his arm, just to reassure him, but feared that he might not appreciate the contact…not when he was so vulnerable.

"I never wanted to be cruel toward the man," Mr. Diggory said, wiping at his eyes with the back of his hand. "It was just… My son, he's gone. All that pain, all that anger, it seemed to spill right out of me. I couldn't find it in me to be kind. All I wanted was for everyone else to feel the same pain I was feeling. If I couldn't be happy with my life, then no one else could, either."

"I know exactly what you mean…" I said in a small voice I wasn't certain he could even hear over the rain. If anyone could understand this man's pain, it was me.

He sniffed once again. "Then I heard the beggar had been killed," he said, seeming to regain some of his composure. "I was shocked. I very nearly convinced myself that it was my hatred alone that had somehow ended the poor man's life…and when I heard that he wasn't even German, I…" he said.

"It was a misconception that many people had," I said. "You weren't alone in that."

"Yes, but how much different could we have acted

toward him if we had known there was nothing to fear?" he asked. He shook his head. "We should never outright hate anyone, just because of where they've come from. I had a good friend as a child who was from Germany, and I have no idea if he's survived all these terrible atrocities that have been happening over there."

He shook his head.

"No matter what side we're all on, this war is a tragedy...and what happened to that poor beggar...no one deserved the fate he endured."

I couldn't agree with him more.

He looked at the grave, the rain continuing to drip off the edge of the umbrella.

"I'm sorry..." he said. "For how I treated you. Perhaps if I had been more willing to try and understand you, your life wouldn't have ended the way it did. I could have given you a room to stay in, and perhaps done what I could to help you find someone who could translate what you were saying..."

"It does no good to dwell on regret," I said. "What's done is done."

"Yes, I know," Mr. Diggory said. "And it is a weight that I will have to bear for the rest of my days."

"Do not burden yourself like that," I said. "How could any of us have known how it was going to end?"

He didn't respond for a moment.

"I suppose you're right," he said. "Nevertheless, I still grieve for his passing. Too many lives are being lost in the war, and now we must experience these tragedies in our own small village?" He sighed. "Sometimes I wonder what good is still left in this world..."

He turned and started back down the path through the cemetery, his footsteps slow and methodic, his eyes glued to the ground.

His last statement lingered in my mind as I glanced at the beggar's tombstone as well.

Sometimes I wonder what good is still left in this world...

12

The end of June came quickly. The rainy afternoons became more frequent, so much so that rain barrels were overflowing, and parts of the road outside town were washing out almost entirely.

Sidney spent nearly a week away from home, trying to work with the men in the village to repair it as best they could. It was a great effort, though, and I caught a glimpse of him returning late one night, covered head to toe in mud, dragging himself from his car back into his house.

The warmth of the summer days continued to cling to the daylight hours, though, and it was rather difficult to find relief. Windows were thrown open until the storm clouds rolled in, and Irene had started selling cups of freshly made lemonade at her tea shop, along with iced treats.

It was very nearly July when the town's festival finally arrived, much to the excitement of everyone around. Flags were hung, the street swept clean, and visitors from all around began to arrive, anticipating an incredibly ordinary, yet whimsical and joyous event.

Many shop owners in town were closing up for the three days that the festival lasted, including myself, though it certainly didn't stop many of the women in town from ordering last minute necessities for their husbands; ribbons for their hats, patches for their trousers, buttons and straps for suspenders.

I was very nearly convinced I was responsible for half the available clothing in town by now.

Irene and Nathanial had chosen to stay open, especially for the first day. It was a wonderful place to get out of the heat or the rain during the festivities, and enjoy a nice break from the crowds.

I insisted on helping that day, of course, much to Irene's dismay.

"You really should be out enjoying the celebration," she said for the fourth time that morning.

"Without you?" I asked, grinning at her. "I couldn't possibly."

She gave me a firm, yet incredibly pleased look as another wave of customers spilled in through the front door.

I delivered orders of iced treats to children and their parents, as well as chilled glasses filled to the top with lemonade. Everyone had smiles on their faces as they left generous tips and departed, ready to spend the rest of their day out in the festival.

I sank down into a chair near the door to the kitchen, hidden away from view of the customers. Picking up a pitcher of water Nathanial had set out for us, I poured some into a glass, and guzzled it down in three, long sips.

The bell sounded over the door, signaling more customers.

"Good afternoon, Inspector Graves," I heard Nathanial say.

The glass in my hand nearly slid down to the floor. I clutched it tightly in my hands at the last moment, my heart leaping into my throat.

"Good afternoon, Mr. Driscoll," Sam Graves said in his gravely, deep voice. "Mind if I have a table in the back? I've got a meeting and would rather not be overheard."

"Certainly," Mr. Driscoll said.

Slowly, I got up from my seat and peered over the low wall.

Sam was alone, but he was dressed for work like he always was. Did the man ever relax?

I watched as Mr. Driscoll led him to the back of the shop, away from the windows where many of the other customers would prefer to sit.

I rolled my eyes. I supposed it wasn't all that farfetched to think that he'd be working on a festival day. I imagined that police work was never really ever finished, was it?

Irene pushed the kitchen door open, and I reached out, grabbing onto her sleeve and pulling her close to me before she made it too far.

"What is it?" she asked.

"Sam Graves is here," I said. "I'd rather he didn't see me."

"What's he doing here?" she asked, her brow furrowing.

"Meeting someone, I guess," I said.

"You mean meeting two people?" Irene asked, pointing over the low wall.

I peered over it, and saw that a young couple had joined Sam at the back table.

"Why would he choose here of all places to meet them?" I asked.

"Perhaps because it is a public place?" Irene asked.

Nathanial appeared around the low wall, making his way to the kitchen.

"Honey, what is Sam Graves doing here?" she asked.

I leaned around her, eager to hear the answer.

Nathanial glanced over his shoulder at the inspector and the couple he was seated with. "I'm not entirely sure, but I asked him if it was something dangerous. He assures me that it's nothing like that...he just had to deliver some bad news to a family."

"Oh..." Irene said, her face falling. "How terrible. Why did they choose to meet here and not at the police station?"

Nathanial shrugged. "Perhaps he thought this might be a better place to share his news, though I imagine the poor family will never want to step foot in here again after they're done speaking."

I stared at the couple. The young woman's eyes were wide with shock, as if she'd already been given the bad news. Had she come here, anticipating what was to be said?

"The Wilsons just left as well," Nathanial said,

pushing open the door to the kitchen and striding through.

"I'll clean their table," I said, getting to my feet and reaching for my serving tray.

Irene's gaze sharpened, but she didn't comment on my immediate desire to help. "Very well," she said. "But don't dawdle."

She knew as well as I did that the Wilsons had been sitting at the table just beside the one where Sam Graves and this young couple were now seated.

Curiosity once again drove me to do what would otherwise be considered rather mad. I realized with a small knot in my stomach, that if I were a cat, I would most likely have used half of my nine lives by now.

I was careful to wind my way back to that table by checking on the other guests, keeping my back to Sam as much as I possibly could. I didn't want him to see me, knowing that he would likely become angry if he noticed me trying to eavesdrop on his conversation.

With a flush in my cheeks, I realized that was precisely what I was trying to do. Eavesdrop.

I set the tray down on the now empty table, keeping my back to Sam and the couple.

I was careful not to clatter the china as I listened.

"...sorry that you had to come all this way," Sam said. "And given all the trouble traveling due to the war..."

"Yes, very trouble," said the young man. "We – how you say – " and he rattled off something in a different language.

I froze, the teacup in my hand hovering just above the tray.

That sounded a great deal like the beggar who had been killed.

Slowly, ever so slowly continuing to clear the dirty dishes from the table, I continued to listen. The young woman had now spoken up, speaking very quickly in her native tongue. I didn't know any Polish, but it certainly sounded a great deal like what the beggar had said when Sidney and I had met him in the street that day.

"What is she saying?" Sam asked.

"I'm sorry," the man spoke, his accent thick. "She very worry. Her father – you know where he is?"

Sam let out a long, low sigh.

I emptied one of the full teacups back into the pot before setting it on the tray, my ears keenly focused on them.

This poor girl...that beggar was her father?

I couldn't even imagine being her right now. Being in a foreign country, looking for him...only to find out the absolute worst possible outcome had occurred?

"I'm very sorry to have to be the one to tell you both this, but he has passed away," Sam said.

The young man's eyes widened. "He – " he paused. "I do not understand. Away? Did he go somewhere?"

Sam sighed heavily.

I knew I was cutting it close, standing here and listening the way I was. Sooner or later, it was going to be evident that was what I was doing.

"He died," Sam said. "He was killed."

The man gasped. "Gone?" he asked.

The woman muttered something, sounding rather frantic.

The man tried to reassure her, but his voice cracked.

The woman burst into tears, and with a glance over my shoulder, I saw she'd buried her face in her gloved hands, sobbing almost uncontrollably.

"How did this – why?" the man asked.

I did not envy Sam the job he now had.

Sam's voice dropped, and the creak in his chair told me that he had leaned forward to speak to them more privately.

"He wandered into Brookminster a few weeks ago," Sam said. "As I'm sure you both know, he couldn't speak any English. One of our townsfolk walked him to the station, and – " his voice trailed off, and he exhaled rather heavily.

"He came to England, looking for wife," the young man said. "The mother of my wife. They separate when running from war in Poland."

*That's who he was looking for...*I thought, my heart sinking.

"Her mother came back to Poland, and we thought that Father would follow," the man said. "But you say he – he is dead?"

"Yes, unfortunately," Sam said. "The autopsy revealed that he must have been starving, given the emaciated state of his body when we found him. It seems he was involved with some nefarious dealings, stealing from those living here in the village. Given the times we live in, there are many who do not take kindly to their belongings being taken without permission. All we know at this time is that he was killed by gunfire, likely when someone in town was attempting to defend themselves."

The young woman, the daughter of the beggar, was weeping softly. I could only imagine how she felt. It wasn't fair, what had happened to him. Even if desperation had driven him to those minor thefts, he never should have met an end like he had.

I turned away with the tray stacked high with melted icy treats and the remnants of sandwiches. My heart heavy, I hurried away from the couple and the loss they now had to grieve.

Irene caught sight of my face as I stepped through the door to the kitchen. "What happened?" she asked, she and Nathanial following after.

"That girl..." I said, setting the tray down with a great deal less care than I typically would, the silverware clattering loudly. "The beggar was her father. She came here looking for him, and Sam had to tell them..."

I swallowed, unwilling to cry when I knew very well that the poor woman out in the dining room needed comfort far more than I did.

13

"How did they manage to find him?" Nathanial asked after I'd recovered myself. "He was entirely alone, couldn't speak a word of English."

"He must have left something along the way for them to find," Irene said.

"The daughter's husband can speak some English," I said. "But something else is troubling me..."

"And what might that be?" Irene asked.

"Sam told them that the beggar had been emaciated when they found him, but that it was the gunshot wound that had killed him. He told them he had been stealing from people in the village, and that some had certainly not taken kindly to being stolen from," I said.

"But he didn't specify who it was, exactly, that had taken the shot at him?" Nathanial asked.

I shook my head.

"So he either doesn't know, or he didn't think it was

pertinent information to share with the daughter," Nathanial said.

"To be honest, there was one person that came to mind immediately as soon as he said that," I said. "At least, after the shock wore off of hearing him tell them this terrible news."

Nathanial and Iren exchanged uneasy glances. "And who was that?" she asked.

"The farmer that Sidney and I went to visit, just a few miles outside of town," I said. "Mr. Cooke."

"What makes you think it was him?" Nathanial asked.

"Because he told Sidney and I that the beggar had broken into his garage, and that he'd chased him off with his rifle," I said.

"But that was before his death, wasn't it?" Irene asked. "Before he wound up dead?"

"What if the beggar returned, and tried to steal from him again?" I asked. "He was found with stolen goods, and that's what the farmer claimed the beggar was doing in his garage."

"Didn't you say he seemed surprised that the beggar was dead, though?" Irene asked.

I frowned. "I suppose he was...but what if he was lying to us?"

"If I were you, Helen, I would leave this to the police," Nathanial said. "I know how terrible it must feel, knowing the poor young woman out there lost her father the way she did...but that is why Sam Graves was meeting with them. He is going to do everything he can to ensure they are given all the information they need, and I know he's a good man, and will do his best to locate the person who committed this terrible crime."

I nodded. "I know. You're right. I really should just leave it to them…"

Irene wrapped her arm around my shoulder. "Come along, dear. I'll walk you home. I think you need some rest, and promise me that you will put all this aside and take care of yourself, yes?"

"But what about the shop?" I asked. "Don't you need my help today?"

"We will be just fine," Irene said. "I'm more worried about you. You look so pale. Have you been getting enough sleep? Have you been eating well?"

"Yes, I'm fine," I said.

I argued with them for another five or ten minutes before I realized I was not going to be winning, and Irene walked home with me.

"I admire you, you know," she said as we made our way along the relatively busy street. Villagers were walking past, evidence of the festival following along with them; I saw a child with bright red hair gripping the long, fluttering strings of three brightly colored balloons, and a young man eating kernels of popcorn that had been coated in something sugary sweet. A father held an overstuffed bear tucked beneath his arm, while his other hand held that of his young son's.

"What do you mean?" I asked.

"Just that," she said. "I have known many people who would run from the sorts of problems you've encountered. When we discovered that your aunt had been killed in your house, I thought for certain you would move out. I expected you to show up one afternoon, your bags already packed, just to say goodbye."

She smiled at me.

"But you've surprised me. Instead of running from your fears, you've faced them head on."

"It wasn't easy," I said. "I was afraid to live there, not knowing what had happened, or who had caused it. I had nightmares of someone breaking in once again, ready to attack me the same way they did my aunt."

"What made you stay?" she asked.

"This place is my new home," I said. "I moved here to get away from the pain of my past, and I was determined to make this place my own, where none of those terrible memories could follow me." I shook my head. "But those memories came along with me, even if I didn't want them to."

"Distance never separates us from our past, unfortunately," she said. "Eventually, we have to face it and just accept it for what it is."

"As I've learned..." I said.

My little cottage appeared down High Street as we came to it, with its lovely honey-colored stone walls and landscaped front garden. I was proud of such a place, and it made my heart glad to know that it was my own.

"I guess I am still wondering, then, why you have been so invested in this case about the beggar," Irene said. "You didn't even know him."

"I know," I said. "Honestly, there are times when it seems ridiculous to me, as well. But I think that the idea of yet another death going unanswered is just...well, it's almost intolerable."

"Because of Roger?" Irene asked.

"Precisely," I said. My eyes stung, but I kept my head down as I unlocked the front gate of my garden. "I suppose it won't make much sense to anyone else, but I realize that there is a very good chance I will never know exactly what happened to my husband on the day he died, and that...it's deeply troubling."

"I cannot even imagine it, my dear," Irene said as we walked along the path to my front door.

"And I know that I should just keep my nose out of it, but I – "

My hand froze, halfway to the doorknob.

The door was already cracked open.

My heart jumped into my throat, and I couldn't move. All I could do was stare at the door.

"What's wrong?" Irene asked.

She noticed the door, and gasped.

"Did you leave it open earlier? Maybe you forgot to shut it?"

"I'm positive I didn't," I answered.

"In that case, we shouldn't enter," she said. "Someone must have broken in. What if whoever was in there is still inside?"

The blood rushed in my ears, and there was a dull throb at the back of my head. "You're right..." I said.

The next thing I knew, I was being dragged back along the road, back toward the center of town. Irene was urgently trying to calm my nerves, but I barely heard anything she was saying.

～

SOMEONE HAD BROKEN into my house. In the middle of the day. During the festival.

"That might have been the best time," Inspector Graves said when we found him back at the teahouse. The young couple had gone, and Irene was the one to explain what we had discovered. "The burglar likely believed you would be away for the day. It isn't all that uncommon for us to hear about thefts happening on days like this, when everyone's attention is focused elsewhere."

"Will you come with us to check the house?" Irene asked.

"Of course," he said, getting up, and tossing a handsome tip onto the table. "Let's go."

We walked back to my house, my nerves singing the whole way. At least Irene had the sense to tell me to get help from the police. I could have just as easily stepped into the house all on my own. And what would I have done if I'd met an intruder with a gun? Or a knife?

Those troubling thoughts kept chasing themselves around in my mind all the way back down to High Street.

Sam was the one to walk up to the door first. Somewhere along the way, he'd pulled out his pistol, holding it aloft as he leaned up against the open door.

His face hardened, his brows knitting together in one tight, thick line.

Then, he pushed the door open and crossed the threshold in one, swift motion, a move that seemed far too graceful for someone of his stature.

I attempted to follow, but Nathanial gently laid a hand on my shoulder, preventing me from going any further.

"Just wait," he said kindly. "We don't know what he might find."

It was an anxious few minutes before the inspector returned. Every second that passed, I worried about hearing the sound of a gun going off, or the frightened cry of someone caught off guard.

Nothing like that happened, though.

The door suddenly being pulled open startled me, making me nearly jump backward into Irene.

Sam's cross face appeared.

"There's no one here," he said. "Though it's clear they were looking for something..."

He gave me permission to enter the house.

The shop seemed undisturbed. Boxes were as I left them on the shelves, and drawers were still closed. It wasn't until I wandered upstairs that I discovered what Sam was talking about.

It was a completely different place. Every cupboard door had been thrown open, and every drawer was either overturned or pulled out so far they were hanging by the hinges.

"Oh, good heavens..." Irene said, reaching the top of the stairs where I was standing.

I could only stare around in horror. The cushions of the sofa were lying on the floor, and the bedding on my bed had been turned down, and boxes from beneath pulled out and opened.

"Whoever it was seems to have left in a hurry," Nathanial said.

"No," Sam said. "They must have been here for some

time. Unfortunately, I've never known a burglar to ever clean up after themselves..."

Irene laid a hand on my arm. "Who could have done such a thing?"

Sam shrugged his shoulders. "I have very little to go off of. Whoever it was did not leave any clues behind. They've done this before."

A chill ran down my spine.

"I wouldn't be surprised if either of the houses beside yours were hit as well," Sam said. "That Sidney Mason lives next door to you, right?"

I nodded.

"I'll have to check with him, make sure that his home wasn't also broken into," Sam said.

"You should see if they made off with any of your valuables," Irene said gently.

After checking my jewelry box, and the drawer in the kitchen where I kept my ration coupon book, I realized that nothing of value was missing.

"What does this mean, then?" I asked the inspector.

He rubbed his broad chin. "I couldn't tell you," he said. "Normally it's any jewels that go first, as they're the most valuable. Next, it's art, like vases and paintings. Nothing like that is missing?"

"No, nothing," I said. "I don't own very much, so I would know right away if something was gone."

"I'm sorry," he said, and I was surprised by the genuine concern in his tone. "I'll have a constable patrol the street outside your house for the next few days to make sure that if the burglar attempts to return, you are protected."

"And if you want, dear, you can come and stay with us for a few days, just until this all blows over," Irene said.

I agreed, somewhat numbly, but my thoughts could really only focus on two different questions.

One, what on earth had the burglar been looking for? And two...was it connected in some way to the murder of the Polish beggar?

14

Those questions haunted me for the next two days.

At Irene and Nathanial's insistence, I stayed with them in their spare bedroom. Their son, Michael, seemed all too happy to have a house guest, someone new to play with. I knew I was safe staying with them, but I couldn't shake how violated I felt, having my home and personal belongings rifled through the way they had been. I knew that eventually, I would have to reopen my shop, have to answer to my customers about what happened. Not only would it be incredibly difficult to talk about, but I wondered how many people would lose trust in my shop in the first place, wondering if it was safe for them to be there.

The more I thought about the break-in, the more convinced I became that it had something to do with the murder of the beggar. Nothing else made any sense to me. Just like the last time I found myself far too invested in a murder, I hadn't exactly been quiet about my involvement.

If I really thought about it, there were likely quite a few people who knew I had been connected to the beggar, at least in a small way. The innkeeper and his cook, Sam Graves and likely several of his officers at the station. Sidney and Irene and Nathanial. The farmer out across town and his wife.

One night, when I was finally able to get some sleep, I dreamt of Sam Graves showing up and arresting me, accusing me of being the one who had killed the beggar.

It wasn't all that farfetched to imagine, considering my involvement. Not only had I stuck my nose in where I shouldn't have time and time again, I had sneaked onto the crime scene, twice. I eavesdropped on the conversation that Sam was having with the beggar's daughter, and I had sought out information from different people who had interacted with him.

Given my incessant involvement, I could easily see why Sam Graves might eventually turn his attention to me, someone who might seem entirely innocent, yet with a great deal of knowledge. I could understand how it might seem that I was simply trying to cover my tracks, even going so far as to ransack my own house to divert suspicion...

None of that was true, of course. But it made me start to wonder if someone was attempting to frame me, or knew about my interest in the case and was trying to deter me from looking any further.

That means I am close to finding out the answer, though, doesn't it? I thought late at night when the rest of the

Driscoll house was fast asleep; Nathanial's snores could be heard all the way down the hall. *And it also means that someone is aware that I am onto them.*

And the only person I could think that might still be responsible for the beggar's death...was Mr. Cooke, the farmer.

It fit the bill, didn't it? The beggar had been shot, and the farmer had openly admitted that he had chased the unfortunate man away with his rifle. He'd admitted that the beggar had been trying to steal from him. It made me wonder if the goods that had been found on the dead man's body matched those taken from the farm.

I was having a hard time remembering exactly what had been with the beggar's body. Had I been able see anything aside from his face? Had there been any goods in the shed with him?

I knew I had likely reached the limit of requests I was able to bring to the police. As much as I wanted to be able to ask Sam Graves what, precisely, had been found with the beggar's body, I knew I wouldn't be able to without drawing even more suspicion toward myself.

I have to do it myself, I thought. *If Mr. Cooke was the one who broke into my house, trying to scare me, then he might not hesitate to strike again...but this time, who knows if he would try and hurt me. I need to catch him before he can catch me.*

"WHERE ARE you off to so early this morning?"

It was Nathanial. I had been doing my best to be

quiet. It was in the hour before the sun would come up, and I worried that if any of the Driscolls were awake, they would stop me.

My face flooded with color as he smiled kindly at me from the breakfast table, the newspaper open in his hands.

"Oh," I said. "I – I remembered there was an urgent delivery that I had to make today."

"Oh, well, I admire your desire to get back to business," Nathanial said.

I hesitated, knowing I was probably pushing my luck, but decided to try it anyways. "Would it be alright if I borrowed your car?" I asked.

"The car?" Nathanial asked, his brow furrowing.

That was it. I'd asked too much. "My client is outside of town, just south of here. It would save me a great deal of time if I could drive out there."

"Well...I suppose there's no harm," Nathanial said, rising slowly from his chair. It was clear he was not all that comfortable allowing me to take the vehicle, but I knew there was nothing strange in what I'd said.

He passed me the keys. "You'll be back with it soon?" he asked.

"Likely within the next two hours," I said with a smile.

Guilt wracked me as I stepped outside, the keys in my hands trembling. I'd just lied to my dear friend's husband, who I cared for as well...and I'd done it as easily as breathing.

There really was something wrong with me, wasn't there?

I pushed aside my guilt, soothing my anxiety with the

promise to myself that I would certainly tell them everything as soon as I was back. If I'd told them I planned to take the car out to the farmer's property, they never would have let me go.

*I will tell them everything...*I promised myself. *As soon as I get back, I will confess to it all, and I will keep out of whatever happens next.*

My instincts told me that this farmer was responsible for more than he admitted to...and his quick dismissal of Sidney and I was proof of it.

Sidney...

As I drove past his house, I caught sight of his silhouette in the window. He was already up and working.

For a brief moment, I considered stopping and asking him to come with me.

I kept driving, though, when I remembered that he, like Irene, Nathanial, and Sam, had asked me to keep my distance from this whole thing. He would just try to talk me out of it like everyone else.

It was still dark when I reached the farm. I knew it wouldn't be wise to drive the car all the way up to the house, but the drive leading to the farm was nearly a half a mile long.

I decided to park it just off the drive in a low divot of a hill, where it could remain hidden away from the rest of the farm. I tucked the keys in my pocket and hurried up the hill, staring out over the landscape.

The farm was just up ahead a short ways, the golden lights from the house already spilling out onto the ground.

I was going to have to be careful if I didn't want to get

caught.

The air was cool, and my boots were slick from the dew on the grass as I approached the farmhouse, doing my best to duck low behind the tall grass patches along the side of the road.

As I approached, I heard the tractor running around the backside of the barn, which was nestled up on the hilltop above the house.

With any luck, that means Mr. Cooke is too busy, and won't catch me, I thought.

I hurried around to the garage, knowing this was the place where the beggar had broken in. It was dark, as were the nearby windows.

I knew I had to try and be quick, especially before my nerves got the better of me. If I was caught, then what happened to the beggar could very easily happen to me.

I tried the door on the garage, and found it, surprisingly unlocked.

As I pushed the door open, it creaked slightly, sending sharp and terrifying needles of fear into my bloodstream.

I forced myself to take long, deep breaths in through my nose as I huddled in the shadows, fighting the urge to take off across the fields and race back to the car.

The building smelled of oil, dust, and stale manure. I wrinkled my nose as I looked around, squinting through the darkness. My ears were perked, ready to catch the slightest change in sound, or any indication of the farmer's wife coming into the garage.

I didn't dare chance turning on the flashlight, fearing that it would alert the farmer or his wife.

I found a shelf along the wall that was stacked with nonperishable goods. Rows and rows of cans and preserved jars of jams, vegetables, and meats sat nicely in lines, organized and orderly...

All except for a row down toward the bottom, which seemed to be missing more than a few cans.

I knelt down and picked up one of the cans, and realized it was canned mackerel.

I thought hard, back to the night I'd seen the beggar's body. Had I seen anything like this nearby?

I couldn't remember if Sam had mentioned what had been found with the beggar, nor if the farmer himself had mentioned anything...

I stood, eyeing that shelf with apprehension.

There was a work table beside it, which was horribly messy compared to the shelf that was so neat and tidy. Old, oily rags were scattered across it, along with a small, opened box of –

Bullets.

My father had a rifle while I was growing up. He'd shown my sister and me how to use it so that we wouldn't accidentally hurt ourselves with it. I'd seen the size of the bullets that he used to go pheasant hunting, and they were a great deal smaller than these.

These bullets...they'd easily tear through the flesh of a man without any trouble.

I reached out and touched one, seeing the way they shone, even in the darkness.

A creaking sound behind me sent shivers down my spine.

"Well, well...look what the cat dragged in."

15

I was certain I had never been so frightened in all my life.

I stood frozen in that dark garage, my heart pounding against my chest so loudly that I thought it would beat right out of my body.

Footsteps against the hard, concrete floor behind me caused my blood to sing with terror, but like a rabbit caught in a trap, I could do nothing. My fingers went numb, and my mind had gone blank.

"When I saw a shadow rustling about in here, I thought at first that it was that despicable vagabond come back to haunt me," the farmer said. He laughed once, a sound that reminded me of a bark. "But then I remembered there was no way he'd still be walking around...it wasn't possible."

"Mr. Cooke," I said, my voice trembling as I slowly turned around, my hands lifted in the air. "I'm terribly sorry. I didn't mean to frighten you. I simply wanted to – "

"I don't care what you wanted," Mr. Cooke said, stepping fully into the garage.

It was at that moment that I noticed the rifle in his hands...pointed straight at me.

My breathing was sharp, coming in hard and fast. Darkness began to press in on me, especially around the edges of my vision.

"What is it about my property that makes all of you people think it's perfectly fine to break into my home?" he asked, his voice rising ever so slightly.

"Mr. Cooke, I just wanted to help. I have been working with the police, and all I wanted to do was help you – "

"Oh, well, this makes perfect sense, then, doesn't it?" he asked. "That day when you showed up here with that Sidney Mason, I thought something was suspicious... especially since you both seemed so keen to talk about that beggar fool."

"All we wanted was to know what happened to him," I said. "His death was so sudden, so severe, that – "

"Well, of course it was," Mr. Cooke said. "What did you expect? When someone forces his way onto a man's property, do you suggest he just allow it to happen? That he do nothing to fight back?"

His voice was rising in volume, and it made my head throb.

I backed into the workbench behind me, the rifle rounds in the box shaking and clanking together as I did.

Mrs. Cooke, please! I thought desperately. *Please come out here and see what your husband is doing, what he might do –*

"I could have forgiven him if he had only come around that one time, as horribly as he acted. I could forgive nearly starving to death and wanting food. Wouldn't it have been better if he had asked me instead? But no. He thought it was best to sneak in like a criminal in the middle of the night, and *steal from my family*," he said, snarling.

My hands were trembling as I tried as discreetly as I could to find something on the workbench that I could use to defend myself. An old blade, a spike, a nail...I didn't care. I just wanted something that could put some distance between me and the farmer.

"You know, I almost felt bad, after everything happened...finding out that the beggar was actually Polish," the farmer said. "It made it so much easier to kill him thinking he was a German."

My fingers scraped across something cool to the touch, something metal. A screw! It was slightly rusted, but a gentle press on the pointed end with the tip of my thumb told me it would do the trick.

"So you admit to killing the beggar?" I asked, easing the screw back toward my pocket, careful to keep my eyes locked on his. So far he hadn't noticed my discovery.

"I thought I already did," the farmer said, furrowing his brow.

His face was even gaunter in the shadows than it had been when I'd first met him.

"Why?" I asked. "Just because he came back to your property?"

"Yes, wouldn't you have killed him?" he demanded.

"No!" I said, anger piercing through some of the fear. "I would have called the police and let them handle it."

"They wouldn't have done anything," Mr. Cooke said. "It wouldn't have made any difference. He would have kept coming back again, and again, and again...just like the enemy. They're like roaches, an infestation, and deserve nothing less than a fiery, burning – "

"Mr. Cooke..." I said. "You used your anger toward the Germans to fuel your hate of that poor beggar?"

"So what if I did?" he asked. "This war is the worst thing that our country has ever had to endure. It has driven ordinary, happy people to the depths of despair, having to experience a drought of peace for yet a second time in such a short amount of time..."

He lashed out, slamming his fist into the wall beside him, causing all the tools hanging there to dance and tremble, a hammer tumbling to the floor of the garage.

"These wars have taken my family away from me," he said, just barely above a whisper. "My son, and his son... both of them were killed by those – "

There was a rather childish sob that escaped him, but it quickly changed into a growl.

"My son, William...bright eyed, wanted to be a doctor...he just had another baby, you know. His wife, Henriette, almost died in childbirth. He was just able to hold their new baby before they shipped him back off to the front lines..." he said.

My heart ached, despite the fear. How was I feeling sympathy for this man?

*Because he is as broken as I was when Roger died...*I realized. *Even still...now is not the time for compassion.*

"And my grandson...just turned eighteen. Handsome as anything, with his whole future ahead of him. He had dreams of joining the theater, performing Shakespeare to the veterans of the war...but now he is gone, too. The life ripped right out of him. And for what reason? Money? Power?"

He lowered his rifle, and I breathed a small sigh of relief.

"I know how you feel..." I said nervously, my gaze still keeping sharp watch on that rifle.

"No, you don't," the farmer said, setting the rifle down against the wall.

"I do," I said. "I lost my husband in the war too. He was killed in one of the air raid bombings in London."

The farmer spared me a quick glance over his shoulder as he walked over to a cabinet along the far wall. "Was he now..." he said, pulling the door open.

"I understand the pain that comes with losing someone you love so dearly," I said. "I understand the fight against hatred, bitterness against an enemy whose face we've never seen, which makes it so much easier to despise them."

"That it does..." he said. "And that's perfectly all right with me."

I heard the sound of something rustling around inside the cabinet, and I wasn't sure what in the world it was that he was doing. He wasn't making it easy to understand.

"Mr. Cooke, I am terribly sorry this all happened to you, but you understand that an innocent life was lost because of your anger?" I asked.

He turned back around, a circle of rope draped over his arm, and a rough sackcloth in his other hand.

My heart began to race as my eyes fell on them. "Mr. Cooke?" I asked, realizing there was nowhere I could possibly go. "What are you – "

"I'm sorry that you lost your husband, but don't fret too much. I can make sure you go to see him soon enough," he said, walking toward me with the sackcloth outstretched in his hands.

I tried to run toward the door back outside, but he was faster; he grabbed onto my wrist and yanked me backward.

Before I had a chance to react, he shoved a cloth between my teeth, and then pulled the sackcloth bag over my head.

I shrieked, but the sound was muffled by the cloth in my mouth. Even as I reached up to rip the bag off my head, he beat me to it, dragging both of my hands behind my back and tying the rope around my waist, pinning my arms behind me.

Panic flooded me, threatening to consume me as he grabbed onto the back of my shirt and began to shove me outside.

I could just see through the thin sackcloth; the horizon was growing bright, the dim light of dawn causing the tops of the trees to appear as inked images on the beautiful grey backdrop.

I wanted to ask him what he was planning to do. Where he meant to take me.

But the answer became quite clear just a moment later.

A stone well, like something out of a fairy tale, appeared at the edge of the garden...and he was steering me right toward it.

"I'm sorry it had to end this way," he said. "But I'm just a simple farmer, who wishes for nothing more than a quiet life. And like I said. I'm doing you a favor. You'll be with your husband soon enough."

I squirmed, trying to break free from his grip, doing whatever I could to dig my heels in and stop moving closer to the well.

"You'll have to say hello to my son and grandson for me, as well..." Mr. Cooke said.

You can tell them yourself —

I was just able to reach my back pocket, and pulled out the screw. With a deft twist of my waist, I was able to graze the back of his hand with the sharp point.

He let out a cry of pain, letting go of me.

I didn't hesitate. I took off back down toward the main road.

My strides were clumsy and my view unclear, but I didn't care. I was much younger than Mr. Cooke, so I knew I could easily outrun him, hands tied behind my back or not.

As I ran, I worked my shoulders and elbows, shifting the rope, loosening the knots.

I just made it to the hill where I'd stashed Nathanial's car when I managed to get the rope loose. I let out a cry of joy and tossed the ropes aside, yanking the sackcloth from my head at the same moment. I spat the cloth in my mouth out and threw myself against the car.

With trembling hands, I shoved the key in the lock... just as I heard Mr. Cooke's angry shouts growing closer.

I wrenched open the door and dove inside, slamming it behind me. It took me two or three times to get the engine to start, muttering to myself underneath my breath as I did.

Come on, come on, come on!

The engine turned over, and I threw the car into reverse, stomping on the pedal. The car flew backwards just as Mr. Cooke crested the hill, his rifle back in his hands.

The sound of the gunshot echoed throughout the still morning, making me scream as I ducked down behind the wheel.

When I lifted my head, I twisted the steering wheel, causing the car's wheels to spin in the dirt, nearly turning it all the way around.

Throwing it into drive, I stepped on the gas and drove away, dodging and weaving through the sparse trees in order to protect myself.

As soon as I was on the road, I realized I'd been holding my breath.

16

"Inspector Graves!" I shouted, panting, as I raced into the police station. "Inspector Graves, you have to come quickly."

One of the receptionists tried to stop me, but I hurried right past her desk toward the hallway leading back to the rest of the station.

Other officers peeked their heads out of their offices, and at the very end, Sam Graves appeared.

"Helen Lightholder..." he said. "What seems to be the matter?"

I staggered to a halt, my strength very nearly giving out on me as I rested my hands on my knees, sucking in breath after breath. "I know – who killed – the beggar."

There was muttering behind me, but I couldn't care less.

"He just – he just tried to kill me," I said.

Sam's face hardened as I looked up at him. "Who was it?"

"One of the farmers, outside of town," I said, my mouth dry and tacky. "Mr. Cooke."

More muttering.

Sam seemed to debate with himself internally. He snatched his jacket from a hook just inside his office. "Come with me, Mrs. Lightholder," he said, throwing it over his shoulder.

We made it to his car, but not before he collected a pair of constables to follow along after us.

Outside, he gestured for me to climb into the passenger seat beside him. The other policemen, I noticed, piled into a separate vehicle.

"Tell me what happened," he said. "Don't leave anything out."

So I did. I told him about Sidney's suspicions about the farmer. I told him about how I'd gone with Sidney to help with the tractor and everything Mr. Cooke had said. I even told him that I'd sneaked into the farm myself to look for clues.

I had no intention of hiding anything, even if he looked at me like he was just about ready to wring my neck.

"I don't even know where to begin," he said. "I could arrest you right here and now for all the things you've done; breaking and entering, interfering with police business, trespassing..."

"I know," I said. "But we really have to get to him. He is grieving the loss of his son and his grandson, and I think it's made him lose his mind."

"That's about what it sounds like," Sam said. "While I won't be arresting you, since your life was in danger, I hope you know that I will not tolerate your interference like this again. Consider this a warning."

"Duly noted," I said.

The farm came into view a short time later, and my heart began to race.

I looked back over my shoulder and found that the policemen following in the car behind us lagged far in the distance. It seemed we were on our own, at least for the moment.

"He has his gun, remember," I said.

"I remember," Sam said. "Get in the back seat, and keep your head down."

I didn't hesitate.

We pulled up to the farm, and Sam pulled the car around. He didn't wait for the constables to arrive but got out of our car right away. His bellowing voice broke the silence.

"Mr. Cooke, this is Inspector Samuel Graves. Come out with your hands held above you in the air. If you come forward armed, be aware that I will not hesitate to shoot."

I waited with baited breath.

A few moments passed, and nothing happened.

"Mr. Cooke, I will not ask you again," Sam said. "If you do not come out, then I will – "

"I'm here, Inspector."

I chanced a glance out of the side window, just my eyes peeking over the protection the rest of the metal body could offer me.

Mr. Cooke stood outside the door to his garage, his hands empty.

"I expected that Lightholder woman would bring you back here…" he said.

"Mr. Cooke, I understand that you are not only responsible for the death of the nameless refugee from Poland, but also the attempted murder of Helen Lightholder?"

My heart skipped. Attempted murder. It seemed so much more frightening hearing it like that.

"I am, sir," Mr. Cooke said. "I will not deny it."

"And you are willing to admit this in a court of law?" Sam asked.

"Yes," Mr. Cooke said. "Just…please be kind to my wife. She had nothing to do with this. She deserves to live in peace. That's all we have ever wanted."

Sam waited for the other police car to arrive, not wanting to put Mr. Cooke and me in the same vehicle in case the farmer decided to snap once again.

Mrs. Cooke came out soon after the rest of the police pulled up, and when she realized what had happened, the scene that followed was horribly heartbreaking. It seemed she was completely unaware of her husband's actions, having lived in blissful ignorance of the beggar's appearance in the first place. As Mr. Cooke confessed everything to her, her confusion and distress were obvious.

Sam took me home after Mr. Cooke had been taken up by the pair of constables. I found myself feeling hollow as we left.

"How do you do this, day after day?" I asked Sam as we made our way back toward town.

He didn't look at me, but there was a definite hardness in his jaw.

"Eventually, you just become numb," he said, simply.

It was what he did not say that haunted me as he dropped me off back at my own cottage.

I swallowed hard as I watched him drive away, knowing that I was safe, even if I didn't exactly feel like it.

I knew I would go next door later and explain what had happened to Sidney Mason. He had been almost as interested in the fate of the beggar as I was, although he would not be pleased to learn how I had placed myself in danger.

I would also have to talk to Irene and Nathanial. I needed to return their car to them, and keep my promise to myself that I'd be honest with them. They were going to be angry...but maybe they would still let me stay with them for a few days, especially given what I'd just gone through.

I unlocked the door to my house, and stood in the doorway, gaping as I stared around.

The same thing that had happened to the upper floor had now occurred downstairs.

The robber had been back.

Drawers opened and overturned. Boxes open and emptied. The till was open, yet not a single note had been taken from within.

I sagged to my knees in the middle of the floor, staring around as if there might be a ghost haunting me.

Why did this keep happening? And what was this person searching for?

I had thought this had something to do with the

murder investigation, that it had been the farmer trying to possibly scare me away from asking questions...but looking around, I wondered if this was something else entirely.

"What in the world do you want with me?" I asked aloud, staring around. "Why do you keep tearing my home apart? What are you looking for?"

It wasn't money. It wasn't my valuables. So what could it be?

I didn't stay. I couldn't. Fear pushed me away, and I wasn't going to try and brave it.

Locking the door, I raced down the road toward the police station. Sam Graves had to know this had happened again...and just days after the first time.

The fear of the violation of my privacy was real, tangible.

But what scared me more was that this person always seemed to be one step ahead of me. I wondered if I would ever discover what this mysterious...and probably dangerous person...was searching for.

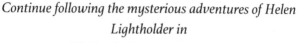

Continue following the mysterious adventures of Helen Lightholder in
"A Simple Country Mystery."

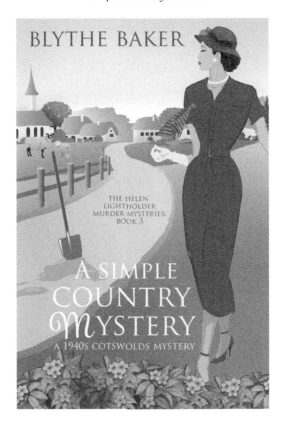

ABOUT THE AUTHOR

Blythe Baker is a thirty-something bottle redhead from the South Central part of the country. When she's not slinging words and creating new worlds and characters, she's acting as chauffeur to her children and head groomer to her household of beloved pets.

Blythe enjoys long walks with her dog on sweaty days, grubbing in her flower garden, cooking, and ruthlessly de-cluttering her overcrowded home. She also likes binge-watching mystery shows on TV and burying herself in books about murder.

To learn more about Blythe, visit her website and sign up for her newsletter at www.blythebaker.com